extremus

a selection of new writing

Edited by Francis M. Thomas,
Bruce Johns, Tammy Palmer
and Nadia Selina

Published by
Imprimata Publishers Limited
for and on behalf of The School of English, Birmingham City University,
in association with the National Academy of Writing

First published 2011
Compilation © The School of English,
Birmingham City University 2011
Contributions © individual copyright holders

The School of English, Birmingham City University has asserted its
rights under the Copyright Designs and Patents Act 1988
to be identified as the author of this compilation.
All rights reserved. No part of this publication may be reproduced,
stored in or introduced into a retrieval system, or transmitted in any
form or by any means, (electronic, mechanical, photocopying, recording
or otherwise, and whether invented now or subsequently) without the
prior written permission of The School of English, Birmingham City
University, or be otherwise circulated in any form, other than that in
which it is published, without a similar condition being imposed
on any subsequent publisher.
Any person who does any unauthorized act in relation to this
publication may be liable to criminal prosecution and civil action.

A CIP Catalogue record for this book is available
from the British library

ISBN 978-1-906192-62-4

Designed and typeset in Chaparral Pro with InDCS5
by Mark Bracey @ Imprimata

Printed in Great Britain

Imprimata

Contents

Foreword by Barry Turner v

The Doorstep by Edmund Bealby-Wright............PROSE 3

A Short Film by Ted Bonham................. SCREENPLAY 15

When the snow lay round about by Jill Charles ....PROSE 29

Cuckoos over the Weald by Paul Costello.............PROSE 37

Bedpan Motel by Bruce Johns ....PROSE 49

The Hills and the Fortune by Fiona Joseph..........PROSE 59

The Sunken Gardens by Derek Littlewood ....POETRY 67

The Boy from Chalk Street by Kate Mascarenhas......PROSE 73

We don't have to carry our Fathers by Roy McFarlane..POETRY 87

Love and Loss by Geoff Mills ....PROSE 97

The Aftershock by Tammy Palmer .... RADIOPLAY 101

Falling Away A memoir by Sean Pullen ....PROSE 121

A Very Long Engagement by Nadia Selina............PROSE 133

Clean-up on Aisle Five by Francis M. Thomas ... SCREENPLAY 139

Delphiniums by Polly Wright......................PROSE 155

The Skeleton in the Cupboard by Suzanne Wright .....PROSE 167

Foreword

This is the fourth anthology produced by the students of The School of English, Birmingham City University, in association with the National Academy of Writing.

Good writing is all about imagination. Whatever is mundane or predictable has no part in literature or, at least, in literature that anyone except for the author's nearest and dearest wants to read. In the work presented in this anthology there is a wealth of imagination, story lines and ideas that cause the reader to stop, pause and wonder. That this impact is hardest to achieve within the narrow confines of, at most, two or three thousand words makes the result all the more impressive.

Where these new writers go from here depends on a measure of luck. Publishing in all its forms is going through a process of dramatic change, forced in large part by the internet and screen reading. But whatever shape the industry eventually takes, creative writing will have its place. The ability to create new worlds for readers to explore will always be in demand whether for enlightenment or entertainment or both. This anthology is a strongly constructed showcase for the next generation of communicators. They deserve our support.

Barry Turner
Visiting Professor, Birmingham City University, Former Chair of the National Academy of Writing and editor of *The Writer's Handbook*.

extremus

Edmund Bealby-Wright

Edmund Bealby-Wright enrolled at the National Academy of Writing in 2007 and his final project for the diploma course, the novel *This Farewell Symphony*, won the 2010 Impress Prize for New Writers and will be published in June 2011.

Edmund has written features for *The Independent* and a series of architectural guidebooks, appeared on radio and collaborated on projects for television. His most recent publication (January 2011) was a children's history of the Black Country.

Edmund is currently working on a comic novel about inheritance tax and a book of philosophical adventures set in the 6th Century BC.

The Doorstep
by Edmund Bealby-Wright

I presume I was born. How else could I be found wrapped in a blanket resting against the boot-scraper at the moonlit doorway of a grandiose mansion (to skip over the details for the sake of brevity) in the small hours, in the darkness before dawn, when births and burglaries occur? The mention of a moonlit doorway puts in mind the poetical notion of a traveller knocking on one of these whilst his horse in the distance neighs and farts and scrapes his hoof on the ground. Was I left here by such a traveller with an impatient yet windy mount? It is an act of hopeless optimism to ask this question since the only person able to answer it is by necessity elsewhere, or else they could not be said to have left me. And besides, where did such an idea come from, since the recollections of a new-born baby would not run to poetry? Unless the knocking was my mother's heartbeat and the other sounds were played on the pipes of her human organ, creating these monotonous memoirs in utero.

I regret the need to go back over the events that antedated the beginning, since the word 'beginning' becomes meaningless when you do this, but the mystery of how I came to be on the doorstep has been the chief preoccupation of my life. If it is solved in the end I shall make that my ending. In the meantime I could speculate endlessly on the identity, purpose, sex and number of the person or persons who played this trick on me. This I won't do – at least not endlessly.

One might be tempted to speculate that my natural mother had abandoned me on the doorstep. A weighty accusation to make of one's own flesh and blood, since exposure of a child under the age of two is an indictable misdemeanour dealt with under Children, cruelty to. It would be simple enough to reconstruct a plausible scenario that might begin with her violation at the rough hands of a stranger; the swarthy impregnation of her alabaster softness, shredless alike of clothing or evidence. Romantic nonsense such as that may appeal to a gallery of soap opera sponges, but there is enough of that sort of thing already, and no need to invent more examples. Besides, it would reflect badly on me, a sprog sprung from such a source. No, I cannot countenance such a beginning.

> NOTE: The alert reader will have noticed that I write in the superb manner. This is because I am a Cockney, born (or at any rate found) within the sound of Bow bells. We Cockneys are renowned for the gorgeousness of our spoken argot, and those of us who can write are unable to resist ornamenting our narrative in order to conceal the deeper meanings of them.

But enough of my local tribesmen: I would much rather write about the design and construction of the doorway where I began. This was no ordinary front door. It was a portal, with Hawksmoor voussoirs and straps of stone straitjacketing the Tuscan columns that supported a segmental pediment, broken in half and the halves reversed to resemble an open book, on which was balanced a huge stone egg; a paperweight mistaken for a bookmark.

> NOTE: The brass boot-scraper was in the shape of Noah's Ark and was kept clean by a footman whose duty it was to scrape all the mud off it that had been placed there by visitors who had arrived on foot. Before the introduction of the boot-scraper, the footman had to scrape the mud directly off the visitor's boots, assisted by the under-boot scraper and the side-boot scraper. The mechanism was therefore a great advance for domestic economy, allowing for the two boot-boys to be given, metaphorically, the boot.

It being the dead of winter, no visitors had ventured out, or at any rate none had arrived, and so the boot-scraper had not required de-soiling by the remaining footman. That is how I came to be lying against the Ark un-noticed for so long. Nutrified through the placenta, a baby has resources that enable it to withstand hardship for longer than a full-born person, prone to hunger, and thence boredom and loneliness.

Further speculation may lead one to suppose that I had previously been inside the house and was taken outside and placed on the step, by a perplexed burglar who had mistaken me for a bundle of valuables and absconded with me only to be alerted by my cries to the true nature of his swag. I imagined him creeping back to the doorstep before skulking off into the night to the little row-boat he had tethered to a nettle on the North shore of the island. Oh yes, the doorstep on which I entered consciousness was situated on a bosky island in the middle of the River Thames, called the Isle of Dogs.

The description 'bosky', though confined to one word and therefore admirable for its brevity, gives a hopelessly inadequate picture of the Isle of Dogs as it was at the time of my presumptuous nativity, at the turn of the year 1962. In that period the district was a derelict spur of land formed by a loop in the river and not an island at all. Just as the Nile water, introduced through an artificial duct, created a moat around the pyramid where Cheops was laid, so there had been plans to give the Isle of Dogs a North shore by making a new channel running parallel to the East India Dock Road, roughly from the Black Ditch to the Lea. If you have any difficulty visualising this, take a look at your big toe. You will see that it is attached to your foot. Taking a sharp knife, sever the toe at this junction and you will see that it is now an unattached oval. That was the intended fate of the Isle of Dogs. These plans were abandoned because, had they been carried out, they would have achieved nothing.

Before long the burglar must have rowed up the River Lea and then up Hackney Brook to the borough of Highbury where he lived with a lot of other burglars. Once again this is impossible to conceive because Hackney Brook was buried underground in 1858, having, for no fault of its own, begun to smell. Although it is less likely that a burglar should make his escape by rowing upstream through a sewer, anything is possible. The watercress beds that once grew on its banks may flourish still in their subterranean habitat. This burglarious beginning, though fraught with impossibilities, cannot be dismissed.

My paradoxical method leads me from breaking an entry to my next explanation; breaking an exit. There are many precedents for escapees leaving infants in odd nooks when the going gets tough. I am thinking of Moses in particular, but there are examples in history of usurpers who explained their humble origins by this device. If you have been brought up by wolves, you might not be too scrupulous keeping in touch with your foster-parents. And if the new king succeeds, his preposterous origin remains in the history books forever. To test this explanation it seems we have to wait for history to be written. I must only conquer empires to make it true.

> NOTE: The paradoxical method opposes opposites and supposes them to be equivalent in a hitherto unseen way. For example; Mozart = frivolity + profundity. It is also admired for its brevity, or, as I shall for its own sake call it; brvty.

All the explanations so far offered for my presence on the doorstep presuppose that whoever left me there intended that I should be taken into the house. This may not be the case. I could have been left out like the empties, ready to be taken away by the rag-and-bone man.

The Doorstep 7

NOTE: A rag and bone man sings a song of which the chorus runs:
>*Enny ol' iron, enny ol' iron*
>*Enny enny enny ol' iron?*

It is sung as raucously as possible and the verse that follows is both tuneless and in Middle-Cockney and is therefore difficult to capture on paper. Rag-and-bone men were still to be found in the early nineteen sixties; many of them doing their rounds with horse-drawn wagons. However they had begun to appear on television, which is a sure sign that something is obsolete.

With relief I shall abandon speculative theories of who left me on the doorstep. Perhaps I was left here for a joke, though none of the proposed candidates was in jocular mood. We must now proceed with the humourless events that followed.

Those who cherish sentimental notions of the innocence of babies may be surprised to learn that before I even woke up on the doorstep, I was arrested by a uniformed police sergeant who had observed me loitering there in a suspicious manner. He cautioned me and got no response, so, having read the customary rights, he carried me in his arms to Limehouse Police Station, hard by, for questioning. I no longer recollect whether I made loud objection or, in constabulary parlance, went quietly.

At the time I was probably too trusting, perhaps a little simple-minded, maybe even a little naïve, but these were the first few hours of my life and I was vulnerable to misleading advice. I relied on the goodwill of others (a habit I have since abandoned) and so if during the following episode I seem unable to defend myself, have sympathy for the inexperience of extreme youth. I did not yet know how to recognise a trumped-up charge when I was faced with one.

NOTE: Limehouse Police Station was one of the more imposing in the metropolitan area. It had been built about twenty years earlier. Architecturally speaking it was buff brick with Portland stone details, showing the last gasp of classicism. It's inhabitants, by contrast, were Early English Gothic.

At first I was unable to assist them with their inquiries for I had not, as yet, acquired the power of speech; my silence was taken for assent; my bawling for remorse. I was swaddled in fish'n'chip paper, the haddocky warmth comforting the sting of vinegar on my flesh. The Ancient Spartans would have approved of the childcare at Limehouse. They steeped their babies in wine to prove the temper of the body, since this marinade toughens healthy babies and causes weakly children to faint and waste away. They did not use vinegar – that is a slur on their wines.

Little by little, my education progressed. I hope it will not be thought ungrateful if I suggest that my arresting officer, Sergeant (or for the sake of brevity; Sgt.) Burly, was not an especially gifted instructor. He did not believe in learning for its own sake; he wanted me to master words so that I could make a full confession, and he had limited resources at his disposal; he showed me the labelled objects he had planted on me, and thus I learned to say diamond brooch, gentleman's watch and cannabis resin. He tried to accelerate the learning process by using and then withholding bribes as an incentive. He spent nine hours a day trying to make me talk, wheedling me with tea and cigarettes. By the age of six I was on twenty a day and drank upwards of forty cups of strong tea but I had not substantially advanced his inquiries. My admiration for brevity must stem from those long hours spent in the stale atmosphere of the interview room, fabricating contradictory fictions to frustrate Sgt. Burly's scrutiny. It was not all work however; I recall that I used to enjoy the morning sessions making faces out of the

The Doorstep   9

photo-fit pictures, identifying a growing cast of accomplices.

The case hinged on what I was doing on the night in question. The Police alleged that I was breaking into a property on the Isle of Dogs. I maintained that I was being born. It depended on your perspective. In order to vacate my mother's belly I had, by definition, to invade some other space.

Like any child I wanted to know who I was and whence I came. I never received an explanation from Sgt. Burly who seemed to make no effort clearing up the mystery of my beginning. I asked anyone I could, mostly fellow Cockneys who had been brought in for passing counterfeit coins at Billingsgate or for disorderly conduct at the Lord Mayor's Show. They were constitutionally unable to admit their ignorance and so I acquired many explanations, only the most plausible of which have found inclusion here.

By the age of ten I had achieved a level of education sufficient to stand trial. I was charged formally with burglary and whilst I had no arguments to offer I was convinced that they had none to counter. Perhaps whoever left me on the doorstep in my swaddles would hear about the sensational trial and come forward. With this hope in mind, I conducted my own defence. This was a very risky thing to do and yet, for someone like myself with natural astuteness and the attractions of youth, it had great advantages. A ten-year-old boy ably conducting his own case produces a certain effect on a jury. He appears to be at one with the lawyers arguing in the well of court, and there is some absurdity in his departure from there to the dock. This effect is naturally enhanced if the litigant's appearance and manner are pleasing, as this pen portrait of me in action is from the Court Papers shows:

> *The accused was on his feet making his opening statement. His appearance at once arrested attention. Short and slight in person, he is relieved from insignificance by a massive*

head, lumpy complexion, a certain puffy rage about the eyes and prematurely furrowed brow... it is the face of a determined boy – a skinhead on the verge of head-butting someone. The voice is one of singular charm and power. High and melodiously threatening, it is an admirable instrument for an advocate.

I was a beanstalk Jack, cunningly evading the clutches of the assembled legal ogres. Hoping to gain victory by causing the court to despair of ever discovering the truth, I swore myself an enemy to that chimerical concept. Unlike my Cockney brethren I did not lie for the sake of personal gain but for self-preservation. Untruths were my exoskeleton; you could even say I was an invertebrate liar.

> *NOTE: Anyone familiar with the workings of the criminal courts will notice that I have omitted the jury from the following account. I have done so for the sake of brvty.*

The prosecuting council opened the case. 'Your name?'
'Unknown.'
'You told the clerk of the court that your name was Tony Lumpkin.'
'I lied when I said that.'
'Then your name is not Tony Lumpkin?'
'No.'
'Can you explain why you gave the clerk of the court a false name?'
'In order to stop him asking me for it.'
He made a note of this. 'What is the name of your accomplice?'
'I did not have one.'
'You told the arresting officer that his name was Askum Yuself.'
'I lied when I said that.'
'What is your occupation?'
'None.'

'You told the clerk of the court that you were a pastry chef.'

'I told him that merely in order to shut him up. He asked too many questions.'

'Will you tell the court how you make your living?'

'My simple requirements are satisfied by the arresting officer; he keeps me in cups of tea and cigarettes in the hope of extracting a confession.'

'You are charged with entering. What were your intentions? Burglary?'

'Certainly not! How could I steal things with no means of removing them?'

'Revenge?'

'Perhaps.'

'I put it to you that you have committed an ordinary break-in for which the object was theft. You confessed as much to the arresting officer.'

'I haven't told him anything. Sergeant Burly couldn't get the better of me.'

'Do you feel any remorse?'

'I do not regret what I have done. But I could not do it again.'

'The arresting officer testifies that you were proud of your deed.'

'I wanted to shock him.'

'You even went so far as to throw a shoe at his head.'

'Certainly, he bored me. That was after ten hours.'

'You will not succeed in this hasty withdrawal of your confession. When you saw the awesome majesty of the court you were consumed with fear and remorse. That is when all criminals tell the truth, before you recovered your presence of mind.'

'Exactly! That is why I replied to the first question by giving a false name.'

My inquisitors found that there was too little evidence against me, and since I persisted in denying everything, nothing could be proved. I denied robbing, I denied escaping, and whilst we were at it I denied the Resurrection. There was nothing left to deny, and if anyone says there was, I deny it.

The case was passed over to the judge who, being obliged to begin his task of summing up without the aid of any cogent facts, gave me a lick with the rough side of his tongue: 'Dost thou think thou canst banter with me such sham stuff as this?' – he screamed. 'God in Heaven may justly strike thee into eternal flames and make thee drop into the bottomless lake of fire and brimstone if I catch you prevaricating in the least tittle!'

I looked up at his now-purplish face in disbelief, but he was by no means finished with me. He placed a black floppy cap over his wig. He meant to bring my life to a close along with the case.

'Your honour... Lord, I am so baulked,' I told him, 'I am cluttered out of my senses. I have not yet begun my life.'

'You have begun badly.'

'Let me continue, then. Is this justice? To appear on the threshold of this great world, without explanation, and to live – to persist rather – in durance, and then after just ten years to have it all summarily ended?'

'Do you wish your imprisonment to be prolonged?' questioned the judge.

'In preference to death, yes.' I replied, in betrayal of cherished brevity.

The judge looked at me with disgust and asked me whether I had forgotten to whom I was talking. 'I order you to be drawn on a hurdle to the place of execution where your body is to be burnt alive till it be dead.'

> NOTE: The reader must bear in mind that this was the very early 1970's and such antiquated attitudes could often be heard delivered in similarly antiquated language though not usually at such fortissimo.

When it was explained to him by a whispering clerk that the death penalty was no longer available, the judge began a volley of wild and whirling epithets, directed at me, of which the mildest described me as a 'Hell-hound' and a 'Judas'. However, despite the judge's threats and coercion, he was powerless against the imperturbable obstinacy of the case, and it was thrown out of court. The Prosecution was prepared to drop the robbery charges, but only on condition that I also dropped my counterclaim that on the night of January the 9th, the presumed date of my birth, I was being born. This was the loophole through which I might avoid further custody, or even, if the Judge had his way; the noose. Therefore, with a bang of the judge's gavel, I was declared a person (or persons) un-born. These unprecedented events assured me a place in the annals of legal history as the first case of a defendant who could claim to be literally a miscarriage of justice.

I was put once more into the hands of Sgt. Burly, and he was not at all anxious to have me back as there was a mutual coolness, as you might expect between gaoler and jailbird. In the 1972 budget the Chancellor put an extra 3p on a packet of cigarettes, and Sgt. Burly put me back on the doorstep. As soon as he was gone I began to look for a way to break in.

Ted Bonham

Wisely, the editors have stipulated that writers should submit their biographies written in the third person. Sometimes a publication will accept biographies written in first person and then attempt to transcribe them into third. This, of course, can lead to mistakes: Ted has a friend, Joey, who once found himself erroneously referred to by the feminine pronoun simply because of his feminist tendencies and gender-ambiguous name. He is glad there will be no such embarrassing incidents in the biographies for this anthology.

A Short Film
by Ted Bonham

IMAGINARY SPACE

The screen is black.

JAMES is here. He has the voice of a young man.

>JAMES (V.O.)
>What am I? I can only see black. Is that intentional or a problem with the picture or something? Well my eyes aren't closed, I can't see the patterns. And why can I hear myself think? It's like when you notice your thoughts so they have to commit themselves to language. I feel like Douglas Adam's whale pondering gravity and a bowl of petunias, or maybe something Kaufman-esque, post modern, a Herzog-style explanatory voiceover perhaps, or a writer listing influences to appear au fait.
>-

A small white dot appears in the centre of the screen. It grows to fill the screen as the voice-over continues.

>JAMES (V.O.)
>- Hang on - O. A white dot. A fullstop perhaps. A light at the end of the tunnel or daylight at the top of a well. It's somewhat difficult to orientate with so little sensory stimuli but at least this feels intentional. Probably the black was supposed to mean something, an abstract absence, and now here I am,

>   this white dot, swelling with the
>   discovery of self. -

A thin black mark appears in the centre of the white, as it too grows it becomes apparent it is text of some sort.

>   JAMES (V.O.)
>   - Wait, there's something more. I can
>   definitely make out something in that
>   white spot. Text maybe, the bottom
>   line of the opticians board. If we
>   strain we might just be able to...

The text suddenly swells so we can read it: "A Short Film"

>   JAMES (V.O.)
>   O. Very droll.

INT. JAMES' LIVING ROOM - DAY

A pair of grey SLIPPERS. They are new but of an old style and have TASSELS on the top. They twitch in and out as they speak.

>   SLIPPERS
>   (in the voice of a
>   young boy)
>   Tassel tassel. Tassel tassel. Tassel
>   tassel.

The room is comfortable and not too too stylish. There is an armchair and a couple of sofas just about crammed in around a coffee table with a bowl of petunias and other odd bits on it. The mantelpiece and bookcase are overflowing, on the former, amongst the candlesticks, incense and vases, is a PHOTOGRAPH of a YOUNG JAMES standing in the doorway of a large, empty room.

JAMES - early twenties, medium build, scruffy bearded student wearing a dark blue dressing gown - is sat on one sofa. MUM - middle income'd and

middle aged and therefore wears her hair short,
she is wearing glasses and her red dressing gown
and drinking tea from a mug which reads "Queen of
Fucking Everything" - is sat on the other. James
looks up at her as she speaks.

                        MUM
     You should write a story, or a short
     film maybe, about those slippers.

James does not seem to register her suggestion.

INT. THE TWO HOOTS - NIGHT

THE TWO HOOTS is the sort of pub that holds poetry
evenings and stand-up comedy nights. It serves
ales, has a model train which runs around the bar
at close to ceiling height and is usually busy.
The clientele range from corduroy wearing old men
to corduroy wearing young students (with some non-
corduroyed patrons inbetween).

James is stood near the bar with JEMIMA FOXTROT.
Jemima is in her early twenties. She is petite,
has short dark hair and wears vintage clothing.
She is holding a large glass of red wine.

                      JEMIMA
     ...remember? you promised you'd write
     me in.

                      JAMES
     Of course.

INT. THE TWO HOOTS - DAY

James is wearing his blue corduroys, a tweed
blazer and his grey slippers. He is sitting alone
at a booth with his black leather notebook, his
fountain pen and two thirds of a pint of ale.

                      JAMES
       (muttering)
     So you'll write me in?

INT. THE TWO HOOTS - NIGHT

Jemima is spinning like a ballerina in a music box complete with eerie music.

> JEMIMA
> ...I have nothing to say, I have nothing to say, I have nothing...
>
> JAMES (V.O.)
> ...I have nothing to say, I have nothing to say, I have nothing...

MONTAGE:

The images flash up rapidly as a DRUM ROLL builds in both speed and volume;

A) Flies stuck on fly paper.

B) JAMES' LIVING ROOM: James, alone, struggling to get the cork out of a bottle of wine.

C) A mouse being caught in a trap.

D) The bowl of petunias.

E) James underwater in the bath.

F) A line of white powder being cut with a library card.

G) A rabbit in a trap.

H) JAMES' LIVING ROOM: James drinking wine alone.

I) Image of Jemima asking about being in the film.

J) Mammoth drowning in a tar pit.

K) THE TWO HOOTS: A party, James is being offered a line.

L) JAMES' LIVING ROOM: James is snorting a line alone.

M) James sits up in the bath, gasps in air.

N) A whale plummeting.

O) Light bulb coming on, then smashed with a hammer - cymbal crash (drum stops).

P) Light bulb comes on -

INT. EMPTY ROOM - NIGHT

- light bulb on. A BUZZING noise. The room is empty, bare walled. James is watching CRAZED JAMES standing under the naked bulb. Crazed James looks like James but is wild haired and wide eyed, he is wearing James' dark blue dressing gown.

The BUZZING isn't the light bulb, it's Crazed James, he is making a noise like a fly. He also seems to be following a fly with his eyes. There is no fly.

Crazed James' buzzing pauses occasionally as if he sees the fly stop. He even seems to lose track of it occasionally. This goes on too long. James begins to grow impatient when Crazed James finally stops buzzing.

> CRAZED JAMES
> (doing up his flies)
> O! Sorry.

James slowly backs out of the room.

INT. THE TWO HOOTS CORRIDOR - NIGHT

James looks up as he backs out of the room. He notices that it is the ladies' toilet. Shaking his head he heads into the men's.

INT. THE TWO HOOTS MEN'S TOILET - NIGHT

There are no toilets. The room is spacious and mostly empty, there is a large round rug which covers most of the floor. There is an empty bowl and two forks set in the middle of the rug. A boy stands near the entrance.

The boy looks like James. In fact this is the
image of YOUNG JAMES that was on the mantelpiece.
Young James holds up a tin of beans and a can
opener to James who opens it as they speak.

> YOUNG JAMES
> Can you open these please. Mum says--

> JAMES
> Yeh, sure.

> YOUNG JAMES
> -- I'm not supposed to talk to
> strangers.

> JAMES
> But I'm not a stranger?

> YOUNG JAMES
> No. You're just strange.

James hands Young James back the opened tin. Young
James moves to sit in the middle of the rug. He
carefully decants the beans into the bowl and
begins to twitch his hand over it in a tiny wave-
like motion.

Young James continues this activity for some time.
Eventually he places his pinky finger in the beans
as if checking the temperature. A little confused
Young James looks back up at James.

> YOUNG JAMES
> I never did understand how microwaves
> worked.

> JAMES
> O. - . Me neither.

James backs away again and heads outside.

EXT. THE TWO HOOTS BEER GARDEN - NIGHT

Typical beer garden: a covered area with patio
heaters, further out picnic tables for summer

months, a few people milling around smoking, chatting.

James joins Jemima and STEVE NASHEF. Steve is tall, has a good beard and the same jeans and t-shirt he's had since 6th form.

The three are sharing a joint.

> JEMIMA
> Bit weird tonight huh?

> JAMES
> Bit lopsided, yeh. You guys are going to come down and see me at some point right?

> STEVE
> Yeh, sure. Anyway Jimmy, what's with the slippers? Is it metaphorical or something? Slippers, slipping...

> JAMES
> ...slippage, yeh, not sure. I think maybe it is, like none of it really sticks, it's all a bit loose you know? I mean the whole thing not just this explanation.

> STEVE
> O, right, erm I thought I was joking, it might be a little tenuous...

James has let the joint go out.

> JAMES
> Can I borrow some fire? -

Jemima passes him the lighter and he lights up again. As he takes a long drag in Jemima turns to Steve.

> JEMIMA
> (discreetly)
> I told you he'd gone a bit odd.

                    STEVE
               (discreetly)
          Well, odder yeh.

                    JEMIMA
               (discreetly)
          Shouldn't we do something?

                    JAMES
          - Yeh to be honest I've been stuck
          at home, not much inspiration see,
          that did actually happen though, the
          tassel bit earlier, I was talking to
          my slippers and my mum did suggest
          that.

                    STEVE
          Okay, okay man, we'll come visit,
          hell, maybe we'll even be able to
          inspire you to write some better
          montage imagery than that clichéd
          underwater in the bath thing.

INT. JAMES' LIVING ROOM - DAY

James is sharing a joint with MATTHEW HALLIDAY.
They are sat one on each sofa.

Matt is another student, he has no beard but
scruffy sideburns. They are both looking somewhat
worse-for-wear.

They pass the joint by just throwing it in the
general direction of each other as they talk.

                    MATT
          ...yeh, sounds good. I mean obviously
          you're a massive pretentious dick
          fuck but I'm a friend so I'd sit
          through it.

                    JAMES
          I did come up with a nice bit I
          thought I might use; "Poetry has the

right to life, life has the right to
poetry, aphorisms have the right to
atrophy."

                    MATT
          Ha, that's actually not bad, you
          should put that in.

                    JAMES
          Yeh, I'll crowbar it in somewhere.

                    MATT
          By the way, why are we in your mum's
          living room? I don't think I've
          actually ever been here.

                    JAMES
          O, right, that. I sort of figured
          keep the settings to a minimum, stop
          it getting too confusing.

                    MATT
          Right, yeh, clarity, you're all about
          clarity. (He draws on the joint) You
          sure your life's interesting enough
          to fill ten minutes though? I mean,
          you may need to add a little spice, a
          bit of action.

INT. THE TWO HOOTS - NIGHT

James and Matt are back-to-back in combat poses
encircled by the rest of the patrons of the pub.

                    MATT
          Let he who is without sin cast--

A pint glass smashes against the side of his head.
ALL HELL BREAKS LOOSE. The guys give better than
they get but they take a few hits, there are a lot
of opponents.

They are briefly thrown back towards each other.

                    MATT
          You've still got your slippers on.

                    JAMES
          Do you think anybody's noticed?

They are back in the fight. A man comes towards
James wielding a hammer, taking a swing he smashes
it into a lightbulb (see image O from montage) and
the man is electrocuted.

EXT. THE TWO HOOTS BEER GARDEN - NIGHT

James and Matt are sat smoking rollies, they look
a little beat up but not too bad.

                    MATT
          I'm not sure that's what I meant.

                    JAMES
               (somewhat distracted)
          Mm, right. Sorry.

James puts out his cigarette on the back of his
hand. YOUNG JAMES looks out from the door.

                    YOUNG JAMES
          Do you really think that was cool?

He wanders back off indoors. James HURRIES after
him.

INT. THE TWO HOOTS CORRIDOR - NIGHT

James catches up with Young James as he gets to
the men's toilets. As Young James opens the door
we notice that it is dark inside. They go in.

INT. THE TWO HOOTS MEN'S ROOM - NIGHT

James reaches for the light switch beside the
door.

                    YOUNG JAMES
        Wait!

Young James disappears into the dark and returns
with the empty bean tin and the two forks. He
places them on the floor outside the door.

                    YOUNG JAMES
                (nodding at James)
        Right.

James pushes the switch. The light comes on in the
room and the round RUG begins ROTATING with them
on it. A noise like a microwave HUM.

                    JAMES
        O, I see. Good job I don't have any
        change.

A microwave PING.

Young James quickly fetches the forks and RUSHES
over to sit cross-legged in front of the bowl of
beans. He sits and looks up expectantly.

James WALKS over and joins him. As soon as he is
sat he has a fork thrust into his hand and Young
James begins SHOVELING beans into his own mouth.

                    YOUNG JAMES
                (with his mouth full)
        Why are you wearing those slippers?

                    JAMES
        O, right, yeh. Not sure. I think
        it's something to do with providing
        some kind of repeating image, you
        know for erm, narrative structure or
        something, ground the whole thing,
        bring it all back round to itself.

As Young James speaks, we realise his is the young
boy's voice that was repeating the word tassel
earlier.

                    YOUNG JAMES
          Yeh, sure, but what's with the
          tassels? Tassel tassel. Tassel
          tassel...

INT. JAMES' LIVING ROOM - DAY

James, Jemima, Matt and Steve are all sat around, they have been WATCHING THIS FILM. Young James looks in from the door.

                    YOUNG JAMES
          Do you really think that was cool?

He walks off.

                    JEMIMA
          Ha! I liked it James, but I think you
          might still owe me a script to be
          honest, Matt's in that one more than
          I am.

                    JAMES
          Mm, you're probably right, but he's
          got such charisma, I mean he's such a
          presence on camera.

                    MATT
          Plus I'm pretty handy in a fight.
          Still not really sure why we keep
          turning up in this living room
          though.-

James' MUM walks in (still wearing her dressing gown) carrying a tray of tea and cakes.

                    MATT
          - O! That's why.

                    STEVE
               (taking a slice of cake)
          Thanks James' mum.

As dialogue continues Mum turns to put the tray on the table, nudging the bowl of petunias towards the edge.

>   MUM
>   Thank you guys for coming to visit,
>   he doesn't have many friends come
>   round, do you James?
>
>   JAMES
>   (muttering)
>   Fuck's sake.

EXT. THE IMPACT CRATER - DAY

Blood, blubber, broken bones - post-apocalyptic, almost. The whale must have fallen from a great height.

As we look closer we notice a shattered bowl, the scattered petunias spell the words "Fuck's sake".

>   FADE OUT

                    THE END

Jill Charles

Jill Charles fits writing in between working with her husband, caring for her teenage daughters and volunteering in the Herbarium at Kew Gardens. Born in Newcastle upon Tyne, she has lived long enough in London to consider herself an honorary southerner; however she will always support Newcastle United.

She won the National Academy of Writing 2010 prize for creative non-fiction.

When the snow lay round about
by Jill Charles

Northumberland 1963

A bitter wind blows across Northumberland from the North Sea, rarely ceasing. It snows every year but the winter of 1963 was exceptional.

It began on Boxing Day 1962 with a few fat flakes, disappointing everyone by falling on the wrong day. The wind had dropped just before it started but when Audrey looked out an hour later, snowflakes were being chivvied from their gentle descent, whisking around the washing-line poles and leafless shrubs. Audrey turned back from the window to see Reenie smoothing her apron over her second best dress, her cheeks flushed and a few wisps of hair astray. Boxing Day dinner was almost as much work as Christmas.

'It might keep up all day, Mum.'

'Oh, I hope not, pet.'

'Jack will want to go soon after dinner, while it's still light. You know what he's like about driving in weather.' Audrey glanced over her shoulder as she said his name, looking toward the kitchen doorway.

Reenie didn't reply, pressing her lips into a line that Audrey knew well. "If you can't say something nice, say nothing" was a favourite phrase of her mother's.

'You get the mash done then, Audrey pet, and I'll carve what's left of the turkey,' she said after a moment.

As soon as they finished eating, Jack began packing the Christmas presents into the car boot.

'Don't bother putting that kettle on, Reenie, we'll be off now.'

The main roads were fine, but as Jack turned into the village the car skidded. His hands flew as he wrestled the wheel. A small shriek escaped Audrey as Laura shot along the seat and crumpled, still dozing, against the car door. Carrie, clutched in Audrey's arms, didn't stir.

'Stop with that fussing, there's nothing to scream about,' he snapped.

They made it to the top of the hill but the wheels span as he tried to take it up the drive to the garage and he had to leave the car across the road in the turning space for the cul de sac. She carried the smaller toddler first, snuggled under her jacket, and managed to get her in the cot still sleeping. The drive was slippery, there were a few inches of snow, and her stilettos weren't helping. She went back and searched for her wellies in the cupboard, finding them beneath the fallen coats and cast-aside shoe heap. Laura stirred as the car door opened and looked up. 'Brrr!'

'Yes, it's snowy, isn't it.'

It was Jack's decision to buy this place and Audrey had been happy to go along with it. His reasons made sense for their future. Buying, not throwing money away on rent. Being able to specify things to the builders. Having their own space, not imposing on Reenie and Leonard any longer. Even if it did mean money was tight for the moment.

They were living at the edge of a small housing estate, still under construction, bolted onto the end of an ancient village. The original settlement was sensibly tucked in close to the Roman Wall on flat land in the lee of the wind. The new houses were built up the side of the hill, so steep that Jack had to chock their car to stop it running back down the drive. The front door was reached by a flight of concrete steps.

Only a few of the houses were inhabited as yet. There was Colette across the road with husband Paul, son John and daughter Angela who was exactly two months older than Laura.

Audrey had hoped they would get on but the toddlers always fought and Colette was so house-proud that Audrey couldn't relax in case a biscuit crumb might fall on the just-vacuumed carpet. A bit further along was Joanie, who seemed very intellectual, with her university professor husband and her children in secondary school. Next door was an older woman, Marlene. Not long after they moved in she had leaned across the fence to feel Jack's biceps. 'Can I borrow your husband? I need to move the television and it's *very* heavy.' Her own husband Arthur was away a lot. Audrey was surprised she hadn't yet been round asking Jack for help with her frozen pipes or some other snow-related excuse. After eighteen months, there was no-one she would call a friend, though everyone was friendly enough.

It snowed for days, on and off, drifting against the garden walls. Sometimes the sun shone, more often it was the snow sky, flat and white. Even when it was cloudy the brightness of the valley shrivelled her eyes. The children squinted as she set them playing in the garden. Once the snowman was built, they took little pleasure in the snow, though she still did. Everything looked so clean and tidy, the mess swept under the carpet.

The drifts grew, driven by the winds until thigh high on Audrey, even with her long legs. The snow combined with the gradient meant that the car couldn't make it up the hill, nor could the pram. Jack had to park the car in the village and make his way up in his suit and heavy overcoat, galoshes over work shoes. Late every evening, always later than he said he would be, though by now she knew better than to expect him home by a given time. The other husbands arrived by 6.30, even those who worked in the town. After three years, she knew what sort of man she had married. A workaholic with a desire for order and tidiness, whose tea and coffee had to be made exactly so. The party boy who courted her gone forever, squeezed out by family responsibility.

Everything was down the hill: the library, the pub, the churches, the doctor's surgery, the phone box, the bus stop.

The house was cosy though, thank goodness for the gas central heating Jack insisted on when they were building it.

Eventually, the travelling shop vans couldn't make their visits. The fishmonger wasn't missed, Jack hated fish. But then the butcher didn't come, or the mobile grocery store.

Short of asking Jack to go out in his lunch hour, there was only one way to get some food in. A path through the woods led to a shop on the very edge of the village – Mr Waugh's. Pronounced Woff, not War. It was a godsend of a store, with basic food supplies. More importantly, there was a post office counter at the back, run by Mrs Waugh. Source of Family Allowance – the only money Audrey could call her own. Jack had the bank account; Audrey prepared the cheques for bill-paying but had to wait for him to sign them.

Another day passed bringing fresh snow, and Audrey realised she had no choice.

She had to work really hard to get the children off for their afternoon nap. They must have sensed her resolve because they fretted and refused to settle for ages, but finally they fell asleep.

A photo caught her eye as she was getting them into their beds. It showed a tiny Laura being bathed by her Gran in her kitchen, when they were still lodging with her parents. Reenie was holding a slippery arm firmly, competently; the baby's eyes were popping at the photographer, Leonard no doubt. "Let me take care of that," she could hear her mother saying, repeated so often when they were living there. Audrey was pregnant again by the time this photo was taken. She could still feel that overwhelming exhaustion of caring for the new baby, with the draining nausea and tiredness of early pregnancy layered on top. "Irish Twins," the maternity nurse had called it, "the new baby will be born before the first turns one."

Laura was the first grandchild, and born on her grandmother's birthday, a precious gift. But they had moved out a few weeks before Carrie arrived. The village was only twenty miles away, but in travelling time it was significant. A bus to town, then a bus or walk to the station, a train, and finally a walk. Quicker by car, but she didn't drive. Visits were confined to Sundays, for roasts and respite.

So, after some time spent staring at the heap of shoes and fallen coats, she extracted some long leather boots, hoping they would have good grip, and pulled them on, followed by her coat, fake fur hat with pom-poms, and sheepskin mittens. Fearful of the babies waking, she didn't look at them again before she slipped through the garage to the back door.

Though Jack had cleared the front steps and a path down the drive, he hadn't gone further than a quick sweep of the back step. Even though it was early afternoon, the snow still had a crust from the previous night's frost. Her first step was tentative, her foot hesitating a moment before plunging through. The snow beneath was soft, pillowed by long grasses and nettles and she had to lift her feet high with each step. Beneath all that the ground was uneven, left as it was by the builders, clods and tussocks ready to catch and turn an ankle.

'Better not fall,' she said out loud, as she picked her way to the gap in the stone wall. There would be no-one passing by for hours, even days.

Every step had to be deliberate, it was going to take much longer than she had hoped. If it weren't for the children, she would have paused to appreciate the shocking in-breaths and the muffled peace, listened for a robin's liquid song, but she pressed on. All she could hear was her own breathing, shallow and faster than normal, the rustle of hair against hat, the swish of parting snowfall.

The snow began packing the gap at the top of her boots, working into the wrinkles of cloth, but she couldn't feel it, everything was freezing. Her thighs were beginning to burn with the effort. Deeper in the woods it was a little easier – Scots pines and hollies had protected their patches, bare branches of oak and elm collected their share. Only in the clearings did the snow reach over her knees. Her progress was better than in the back garden until she came to the playing field and hit the deeps again. At the far end, set into a stone wall, she could see the red of the postbox, and above that, a light from the small side window of Mr Waugh's shop.

The path was cleared from roadside to door. It had been salted but as she reached the edge her feet slipped and she teetered into the shop. For a moment, she was incoherent with cold and relief. She stuffed the mittens into her pockets.

First, cash. She made straight for the Post office counter. and handed the narrow book over to Mrs Waugh who stamped it emphatically, then slid it back with the money. Audrey fumbled it into her cold purse, rapidly calculating, the clasp burning her fingers as she snapped it closed.

'Gosh it's taken me forever to get here, I must get back before it starts again!' she said to avert a long chat.

She turned and headed for the glassed display of bacon and dairy. She could afford bread, butter, milk, some cheddar and a few rashers. Mr Waugh took his time, wrapping each item neatly. She had to turn away to hide her impatience, studied the shelves of dried goods, and added some marmalade to her bill at the last minute.

Then she pulled her hat down hard, tugged on the mittens and departed. An icy breeze hit her full in the face, fresh from the Arctic and filled with the no-smell of snow. The sky had darkened while she was in the shop, with the featureless white that said there was little time before the next blizzard arrived.

She skittered across the frozen pathway and back up the slight incline into the playing field. It seemed quicker on the return; she could walk in her old footprints. In next to no time she was into the woods. The wind whipped between the tree trunks and she hurried but took care with every step.

'Mustn't fall.'

A hail of tiny snow pellets stung her face as she reached the flatter part of the woodland path and with her head down she almost walked past the gap in the stone wall.

The deeper snow in the back garden again slowed her. She strained her ears but could hear only the wind roughing up the branches.

Finally she reached the back step. She fell in through the door, catching her knee on the frame. Past the washing machine bolted to the concrete garage floor, up the two steps and into the kitchen. Her fingers could barely bend. Off with the boots, zips stiff with ice, snow like white caterpillars falling from the creases of her trousers. Her toes were numb.

The children were still sleeping, they hadn't missed her. The radio, always on, had covered her absence. She resisted looking in on them, knowing their sixth sense would wake them. She filled the kettle and began giggling. It had taken an age and her limbs would ache the next day but she had done it, there was milk for Jack's coffee.

Though tears began to scald her cold cheeks she couldn't stop the laughter. She pressed her hands across her open mouth as it turned to sobbing and tried to hold it back.

She had never missed her mother more.

Paul Costello

Paul Costello's leading project is a Fawlty-inspired memoir of his days running a Bed and Breakfast. He has written for musical theatre, and is developing a comedy review and one-act plays for local am-dram, featuring internet dating and The Big Society. Though driven by the nonsense of life, his work often reflects the situation for less fortunate people. His favourite source of material is phone conversations on trains, and when not writing he works for Herefordshire Libraries.

Cuckoos over the Weald
by Paul Costello

Bill Tipping shot for goal. Holding off a lanky Italian defender, he took two short steps and caught the round flint perfectly on his instep. On darker mornings he might have seen sparks for his effort, but not at this time of year. Game over, as the stone escaped into thick swathes of cow parsley lining the narrow lane.

Bill loved his walk to the small country station. Nearly forty years and he had no intention of packing it up, enjoying the routine, happy in a community which thrived on familiar faces and warm welcomes. A woman driving her children to school hooted and slowed to edge past on the narrow lane; Bill glared, until he recognised her from the cul-de-sac development at the edge of Heddingly, and waved back.

A cuckoo called from one of the coppices dotting the Sussex Weald, the same bird, he thought, that led the morning chorus he'd listened to from bed earlier. Blackbirds and sparrows foraged for grubs under the high hawthorn hedges. Bill pictured their unguarded chicks as prey for cackling magpies in search of an easy meal. How he hated that sound.

His tinny pocket radio had promised another fine June day. The sun was already high and he felt overdressed in a fleece, but with fickle British weather it was best to be sure. Strapped across his chest, he carried a beige, army-style haversack. Inside were the Coach and Bus magazine, a sticky bottle of sun cream wrapped in clingfilm, and his Tupperware lunch box containing sandwiches, a banana and a chocolate bar.

'Morning, Bill,' called a passing cyclist. 'Lovely day.'

'Morning. Yes – beautiful.'

Bill liked getting there early to watch for the train from the road bridge. Looking down at the unmanned station he could see he was the only passenger. He closed his eyes, savouring the silence and breathing in the crisp, early summer air. According to his Ingersoll watch, a present from his mother and still going strong after twenty five years, the train was due, so he made his way down to the yard and on to the platform, hoping it wouldn't be delayed again.

From an upstairs window in the house attached to the station, a lady with a matronly smile called out;

'Lovely day, Bill.'

'Morning, Mrs Perry – beautiful day.'

Vanessa Perry had lived in the old station house since it was sold off by British Rail. The cosy Victorian charm and pretty cottage garden hadn't gone to waste. A self-taught gardener, she had built a thriving small nursery business recycling garden plants to local enthusiasts and passers-by. Her husband George was more a craftsman than a handyman, his carpentry skills much sought after locally; word of mouth meant he would never retire.

She vanished from the window and re-appeared soon after in the side garden to hang out her washing. She had a knack of putting Bill at ease.

'Train late again?' she called, draping a scarlet sheet across the blue nylon line.

'Disgraceful!' said Bill. 'It's always late. You gardening today, Mrs Perry?'

'Just pottering, Bill. Always something to do, you know, especially this time of year. All those weeds from the railway, that's the trouble – keep blowing over. Some of them are pretty – have to watch the buddleias though. Where you off to today then?'

'Eastbourne– look at the sea, go on the pier. Such a nice day!'

'Sounds lovely, Bill. See you later.' Mrs Perry disappeared into the house with her empty wicker basket.

'Yes, see you, Mrs Perry,' Bill called after her.

He glanced at his watch. The 9.30 train was already ten minutes late. It's a wonder they ran at all, with so few passengers and the local bus cheaper. At Brighton station a year before he'd seen new electronic screens, but here there was no information and no announcement to confirm where the train was.

Standing at the edge of the platform gave Bill a better view up the single track. He remembered the days of steam, when a tiny plume of smoke and the resonant chug of engine exhaust downwind announced the train's arrival. Now, with diesel trains, you relied on eyesight and a mysterious clicking in the rails.

'Come on, come on – bloomin' train,' he muttered, pacing and peering, turning his ear to the wind. 'Where are you?'

He settled on a shady wooden bench and looked at the familiar surroundings. The down signal stood at red but would change soon enough with the train's arrival. Hanging from the handsome Southern Railway station canopy was a slot where the wooden destination boards had fitted. He pictured the stationmaster, Bob, pulling out the old board with a flourish once the train had departed, and slotting in the next one with a thud. Half a dozen plank-like boards, neat black lettering like road signs, were once stacked vertically against the waiting room wall, dealing with all destinations. Not that there were many; Eastbourne in one direction, Heathfield in the other for local trains, and a few distant locations like Tunbridge Wells or even London.

Bob had taken great pride in tending the flowerbeds and pots, applying an occasional lick of paint to the railings at the back of the platform, now hidden by ivy, and sweeping, ever sweeping, with a soft, wide-headed broom borrowed from indoors and guaranteed not to last long on the hard stonework. Chronic arthritis had forced him to retire early, not to be replaced, and as a widower he'd found it hard to cope on his own. After he'd moved into a care home, the house had stayed empty for several years before the Perrys moved in.

Across the track was a space where an old wooden platform

had once stood, a private one with its own electric trains used for deliveries to the hospital Bill had known since childhood. Closed for five years and now lying partly derelict, there were plans to convert the hospital to luxury accommodation, and the only evidence of the railway was a rusting cast iron pole for the overhead cables.

9.53. Twenty three minutes late. It's not right, Bill thought. I'm a regular rail user. I'm on time, so why can't the train be? Frustrated, he paced along the platform edge, kicking hard at a crumpled can until it flew onto the track. He had no time for litter louts – wasn't going to clear up *their* mess. Past the end of the platform he could see the old sleeper-lined coal bays, black stains on their wooden sides and pockets of coke dust amongst the weed-filled bases long after local merchants had ceased using them. Back then lorries would plough back and forth serving nearby villages and the hospital, their sooty drivers happy to trade gossip and weather forecasts with waiting passengers.

10.06. Thirty six minutes late. Bill wrote the morning's readings under previous records in his small, lined notebook. If only they were able to announce cancellations he'd know what to do, but like this he had a dilemma. If he left to get the bus, due in ten minutes, the train was sure to appear on his way to the bus stop. If he didn't, the next bus was two hours. He simply had to wait and hope it would come.

Feeling warm, he returned to the shade and slid off his haversack. Breakfast had been early, so he was already peckish. He unclipped the lid of his lunch box and peeked inside the thick-cut, neatly sliced sandwiches. Cheese and Marmite – his favourite. No harm starting. Chewing on the moist, white bread, he felt a vibration through the platform and tensed to get ready. Then a lorry with hundreds of steel building rods bounced over the narrow road bridge, and Bill sat back again.

Finishing two of his four sandwiches, he ate one stick from the Twix bar and put the box to one side for later. The sun had moved round, warming his back through the thick fleece. Noting "10.29, fifty nine minutes late", he decided there was time to rest his eyes for a moment.

He recalled all the trains that had worked this line. The small saddle tank push-pull steam engines when he first started trainspotting; then the diesel-electric multiple units in the sixties; and now the blue and green carriages, not drab and draughty like the early ones, but all clean and bright and gliding silently.

* * *

Now at last Bill heard the telltale clicking in the rails, faint at first, then steady like a pulse. The signal turned to green as the train approached, and Bill gathered his things, making a mental note of 10.52 to write in his book later. He'd check with the inspector whether this was the 9.30 running late or the 11.00 early, when he registered his complaint.

With a loud belch and a challenging rev the train pulled away from the station, a skinny strand of blue smoke spurting from the exhaust somewhere on the carriage top. Inside, voices were raised to overcome the noise, and eyes flickered shut with the pulse of wheels on rails.

De dm de dm, de dm de dm,
De diddley dm, de diddley dm,
De dm de dm, de dm de dm,
Diddley dm, de dm de dm ...

He could hear the ticket inspector making his way down the carriage. He loved mimicking his friendly banter.

'Tickets please. Any more tickets? Tickets please. Lovely. Thank you, madam. Ticket please, sir. Thank you. Any more tickets? Thank you. Thank you very much. Lovely.'

'Your ticket please, sir,' said the stocky man.

Bill flicked through each section of his scuffed leather wallet, burrowing through scraps of paper with scribbled notes and tiny newspaper cuttings, pulling some out as if they might be hiding the little carded ticket he'd bought at the station. He began to panic.

'It's here somewhere,' he said, elbowing the lady next to him as he switched the search to his coat and trousers.

'I'll come back, shall I?' said the man after a while, too loudly for Bill's comfort and with a hint of scepticism. Bill was aware that the carriage had gone quiet, and newspapers had been lowered to observe the developing conflict.

As the inspector continued down the carriage, Bill rummaged anxiously through the tight pockets around the outside of his haversack and into the deeper ones inside, releasing a whiff of banana and cheese as the contents were disturbed. Of the train ticket there was no sign.

In desperation he scoured the grubby floor at his feet and bent down in the tight seat to feel around underneath, nudging the lady, who conspicuously moved her legs away as Bill invaded her space. The search was in vain.

Having completed his duties further down, the inspector was striding back, his eyes firmly fixed in Bill's direction. Bill saw the sadistic smile of an executioner. Sleeping passengers were nudged awake to witness the drama, and as he got closer the carriage grew quiet again.

Then Bill decided to run. He ran and he ran, down the central corridor, faster and faster – now stumbling – now banging against seats and suitcases – passengers jeering and heckling as he tore past.

As the train pulled into a station, Bill grabbed at the door, but seeing the inspector moving menacingly towards him, instinctively turned and lashed out, feeling his fists thud ineffectually into the man's thick uniform.

**

'Get off me!' yelled Bill. 'Leave me alone!'

'Steady!' said Graham, grabbing at Bill's flailing arms. 'You'll do me an injury.'

Bill started awake but continued hitting out at Graham.

'What's up, Bill?'

'Dreaming – they were chasing me – on the train,' said Bill. 'But I got off. Sorry.'

'That's all right,' said Graham, sitting alongside, wondering if Bill had skipped his medication again. 'Thought you'd be here.'

Hungry once more after the nap, Bill reached for his box. In the sun the remaining sandwiches had curled and crisped like the top of a bread and butter pudding, but the sweating cheese, marinated in melting Marmite, was delicious.

'Twix has melted,' he said.

'That's okay,' said Graham, 'It'll go in the fridge – be fine later. I'll have your banana if you don't want it. Plenty more at home.'

'Hello Graham,' said Mrs Perry from the platform gate. 'He's been all right. We were talking earlier. Fell asleep I think.'

'Yes, dreaming,' said Bill.

'I'm not sure falling asleep in the sun was a good idea, Bill. You're very pink on one side. Forgot to put your sun cream on again. Thanks for keeping an eye out, Vanessa.'

'That's all right, dear,' she said, removing her dry washing from the line. 'He can sit on the platform any time. He's always liked the trains – haven't you Bill? A lot of them have, over the years, you know. It's nice they can be a bit independent, especially after they had to leave the hospital. They not at the Centre today?'

'No, it's closed for a fortnight so they're at home, taking day trips. Might drive across to Hastings tomorrow if it stays like this.'

'That's nice. Don't want to be stuck indoors.'

'Not really! They like it at the house, but get on top of each other after a while. If I wasn't next door, they'd be up to all sorts!'

'Won't see you tomorrow then, Bill. Have a lovely time,' said Vanessa.

'You too,' said Bill enthusiastically. 'Have a lovely time.'

Bill and Graham sat quietly as Mrs Perry wandered off, jobs done. A field mouse scurried to its home deep in the platform side where bricks had fallen away. A pair of contented pigeons noisily tidied their loose nest in the dilapidated canopy roof. Spindly dog-daisies threw fresh seed into cracks in the platform, and butterflies decked the buddleias growing freely in the gravelly edges of the old track, radiating their honey aroma in the afternoon air. House martins fluttered in and out of a muddy cone high on Mrs Perry's wall.

Bill kicked out at small pebbles as they headed back up the lane to Beech House, a converted Victorian villa with interwoven Virginia creeper and a pink rambling rose. On the way they met Colonel Young, taking his afternoon constitutional.

'Afternoon Graham – hello Bill,' said the Colonel. 'Splendid day!'

'Yes, lovely day,' said Bill.

'Been to the station, old chap?'

'Yes – no trains though,' said Bill.

'No trains? Oh, jolly rotten luck. That Beeching fellow! In his own back yard too, eh? Some talk about reopening it. Bit of a long shot, I'd say. Too long ago.'

The blast of a passing white Transit van, using the lane as a racetrack, forced the trio into the verge.

'Slow down, you blighters!' yelled the Colonel, waving his stick after them. 'Need locking up, damn vandals!'

Graham flinched at the suggestion, but realised that the Colonel had led a different life.

'Ha! Blighters!' said Bill. 'Damn blighters!' and was still muttering this as they continued up the lane.

'The others have started the train jigsaw,' said Graham, as they approached the house. 'It looks complicated.'

'No, not without me! They know I wanted to do it!' said Bill, racing ahead. 'Blighters!'

Three backs were hunched over a large board on the dining table, the main feature of a three thousand-piece puzzle starting to take shape. Bill barged between them and grabbed at some unused pieces.

'It's not fair! Shouldn't have started without me!'

'Been trainspotting, Bill?' said Duncan, who'd always got on well with him.

'No trains,' said Bill. 'Saw Mrs Perry though. She's got pink knickers.'

'Yeah? How d'you know that?' said Malcolm, making them all laugh.

'On her line,' said Bill.

'Do you mean her railway line?' said Malcolm, pursuing a joke which nobody seemed to understand, especially Barry, who was more withdrawn than the others.

'Hastings tomorrow,' said Duncan, 'look at the fishing boats; see what they've caught.'

'Won't have caught a train, will they?' said Malcolm tiresomely, peeking at Bill who said nothing.

'Thought we'd stroll up the old railway path before supper – such a lovely day,' said Graham, filling the kettle for afternoon tea. 'What do you think, guys?'

'Good idea,' they all said in turn.

'Better watch out,' Bill added, 'The non-stop to London comes through at six o'clock.'

'This bit's obvious,' Malcolm said trying in vain to jam a green, featureless jigsaw piece into a section of the puzzle.

Bill watched alongside, eyes flicking between the jigsaw and Malcolm. The corners of the piece started to bend up, the green tearing away from the card. Bill had had enough.

'That's not funny!' he yelled, shoving into Malcolm. 'You're not funny at all! You know it doesn't go there!' He lunged across for the limp jigsaw piece, which Malcolm held away laughing, making Bill push him harder and shriek with frustration. The others moved out of the way.

'Can't have it.' said Malcolm. 'Just 'cause you think you know everything about trains. Least I've got proper friends. Poor Mr Train Man – no friends.'

'Give it here!' Bill screeched, grappling with Malcolm.

'Okay you two,' said Graham, 'no fighting. Come on Malcolm – give it to Bill, please. He knows where it goes.'

Malcolm handed it over with a smirk, and Bill gradually composed himself. Carefully flattening down the frayed corners, reshaping the piece as best he could, he set it instinctively into the boiler casing of the steam engine taking shape before them.

Glancing at Malcolm, he patted the jigsaw triumphantly. 'There,' he said, '34045 – Southern Region West Country Pacific – *Ottery St Mary*. That was *never* late.'

Bruce Johns

Bruce Johns recently had a big birthday, and made an equally big decision: to quit work and focus on writing. You will be the judge of whether this was such a good idea. Hitherto he had worked in higher education for a number of years and old habits die hard: he still has a soft spot for accuracy of language, correct use of the apostrophe and words like 'hitherto'. He has featured in all the previous Anthologies but this collection is his first experience of editing. You can be the judge of that as well.

Bedpan Motel
by Bruce Johns

In the year in question I was... well, let's say much younger. That's not forgetfulness on my part, or vanity. Call it superstition, born of long years in the trade. If I say how old I am the phone will stop ringing. The parts will dry up completely. But no doubt you have ways of finding out such things. Or more likely, you'll ask my daughter, who has much less reason to be coy about her age. Although she must be getting on a bit, perhaps to the point when her own parts are drying up, if you get my drift. The Change, isn't that what they call it? Ridiculous euphemism. And ironic, when you come to think of it. For an actress, I mean.

Let's start again. It was never-mind-which-year and Flic was only a few weeks old. Oh yes, that's what we called her, short for...its longer form, anyway. It used to amuse me how people gave their children perfectly decent names and then immediately mucked around with them. Then, low and behold, I went and did the same. Of course, you'll know Flic by her stage name... which eludes me, for the moment. Would have been nice if she'd kept mine. We are a dynasty, you know. Three generations. Or is it four, now? Makes one proud – and humble, of course. Yes, that's it. Humble *and* proud.

I'm wandering, aren't I. Back to the script. It's hard to believe but in those days I was a jobbing actor, learning my trade, not living off the Old Man's reputation. No help from that quarter, selfish bastard. It was a hand-to-mouth sort of existence. In and out of rep. The odd commercial. Parts in films that were only one up from being an extra. I was between roles at the time of this particular episode, but certain the big break was only just around the corner. A little self-centred, probably, but you have to be, don't you? Flic's mother was Penny, who went on to marry... but I'm not giving that *egregious* ham any free publicity. Even in the grave.

You're pulling a face, aren't you, and trying to hide it with your hand. Well, I know it's a slow start but you're going to need some background, some of what Johnny once called underlay. Or was that Larry? I knew them both in their later years, and was even spoken of as their successor. Too much time spent chasing the dollar for that to happen, or so I'm told. Theatre is art in this glorious little country of ours, and cinema is part of the export drive. That's how I got a gong, did you know? Not for my genius, but for services to the *industry*.

No, you're right, that's another story. The incident in question, the anecdote you're not paying me to divulge, I suppose, occurred after we visited my mother. She hadn't seen Flic yet, and was put out that Penny's family had got in first. Even worse, that the Old Man had stolen a march and dripped his poison into her innocent little ear.

The trip from London to the Lakes took forever. We were driving an old Simca. Piece of junk, really, with an engine like a sewing machine, but quite plucky in its way. Quite game. By the time we arrived Flic was wailing pitifully. You know that noise babies make, like cats screwing. They sound so *bloody* ungrateful to be alive.

"Not a very happy little girl," mother said, a whole lifetime's disapproval distilled into one throw-away line. She was always there, upstage if you know what I mean, making light of my success. Quite spurs one on, having a parent like that. What, an Oscar not good enough for you? Then how about a knighthood, a fucking K for God's sake?

I'm sorry. That is no language to be using with a lady. One's standards have slipped along with ... Wash my mouth with soap and water.

By the way, is that piss I can smell?

To resume. The crying went on all the while we were there.

Through meal times, during the night, when neighbours called round. Everyone had advice, dispensed with that slight sneer of superiority that women reserve for new mothers, and none of it worked. The only respite came with movement. Put her in the car, turn the ignition on, and she fell instantly asleep. Stop, even at traffic lights or to let a Cumbrian sheep shit in the road, and she started up again. We drove around the Lakes, the four of us, enjoying the scenery and the silence. No hardship, of course, it's all very beautiful. But a certain tension exists when you're afraid of having to brake. Like that film, with what's-his-name in, where the bus has to keep going or a bomb will explode. Speed, yes, thank you. Keanu Reeves, thank you once again. No, I hadn't forgotten, those stories about my memory are quite untrue. I have always suffered from amnesia when it comes to other actors' names.

Where was I? Oh yes, the visit. It was otherwise memorable for the playing out of old tensions, like lines in a long-running show you can't bring yourself to leave. Mother was still touchy in the extreme on the subject of the Old Man. Was he still with That Woman? Had his looks gone yet? On a scale of one to ten, how dead was his career? I fell into the trap of answering, which she took to mean I saw him often, which in turn implied that I preferred his company. How she sulked. That is when she wasn't complaining about my diction. "You do mumble so," she would say, "I can't see how anyone hears you more than five rows back. In my day..." I always said it was her hearing, although to be fair I was experimenting with natural speech at the time, very avant garde for someone with my background. This was just before The Godfather came out and made it famous. I relied on technique, but they say he put stones in his mouth – him, the one who played ... No, don't tell me. It will come back. Some people are just too famous to be forgotten, no matter how hard one tries.

Anyway, the time came for us to leave, which we did with the usual mixture of guilt and relief. She was a lip-kisser, my mother, highly disconcerting, particularly for Penny, who had to steel herself for any form of intimacy. Let's face it, I should know. Flic was of the same mind, it seemed, her little face screwing up at the touch of that dry, loveless mouth. They got on rather well in later years, or so I'm led to believe. Shared interest in talking about me.

You know, I'm sure that's piss. Can't you smell it too? I have stayed in some of the world's greatest hotels, and let me tell you as a room fragrance this leaves a lot to be desired.

Mmm? Oh yes, the story. We drove back down the A roads, occasionally ducking under the motorway, which was out of bounds to our little jalopy. Progress was good, even so, to the sound of that weedy motor like a needle pecking very fast. But on the outskirts of Birmingham there was a rise in volume, accompanied by a throatiness that was rather pleasing to my ear, like the Ferrari I drove in… You know, the Bond film where I played the villain and ravished that woman with the chest. She didn't take much ravishing, I can tell you.

"That's the exhaust," Penny said. It was her car originally, and although she had been relegated to the status of named driver she still claimed a more intimate understanding of its workings, its *innards* as mother used to say.

I opened my mouth to disagree but was interrupted by a sudden bang from beneath the car, followed by a loud metallic scraping.

"What did I tell you?" she said.

Have you any idea how irritating those words are? I mean, have you any *fucking* idea? Sorry, sorry. Soap and water. But if there's one thing I can't stand it's "I told you so." Gets my goat, even now.

It was Sunday, which in those days meant nowhere was open. There was nothing for it but to hole up for the night and find a garage in the morning. We limped off the main road as soon as possible and drove around looking for somewhere to stay. You are too young to remember how *quiet* Sundays were then. The racket we were making! Like a fart at a funeral. The change in speed, and maybe the noise, woke Flic up and she added her petulant little screech to the din. By the time we pulled into the car park of a pub things were getting a tad fraught, I can tell you.

I don't remember the name of the place, but it advertised rooms and didn't look too squalid. Of course, this being the afternoon, the bar wasn't open, and we had to stand in a dingy corridor shouting "Hello?" before anyone came. The woman looked grumpy at being interrupted – there was the faint whisper of a television from somewhere, and she was brushing crumbs off her dress. You're writing that down, I see, how sweet. It's pure invention, of course, a little detail for the purposes of colour and characterisation. One learns these tricks from the great writers one has worked with. It's a secondary skill, mimetic rather than learned. Like plastering for a plumber.

I'm sorry, I've lost my thread again. Oh yes, thank you, the pub. She had a room, the landlady, and we got her to lower the price. I think she was distracted by Flic, who was now crying furiously. Women have the maternal instinct, it goes without saying, but they also do dislike of children much better than men. We feel obliged to pretend. There was no sense of curiosity as to why we needed somewhere on a Sunday afternoon, but Penny felt compelled to satisfy it anyway.

"We had a problem on the road," she said.

A pencilled eyebrow may have arched its back, but otherwise there wasn't a flicker of interest.

"In fact," I chipped in, "you may be able to help us. Is there anywhere around here that we can get an exhaust system?"

Her face underwent a dramatic change. Both eyebrows were now aloft, and a look of surprise, bordering on alarm, took over. For some reason, she glanced at Flic, still howling, and then said:

"I suppose you could try Citizens' Advice."

We laughed about this when we finally got to our room, but at the time there was an uncomfortable silence. It may be hard to believe, but in those days Birmingham was the centre of what used to be called the British car industry. I had visions of assembly lines on every corner, spare parts hanging from trees. I certainly wasn't expecting to be directed to a help desk for old ladies or people with fucking mortgage arrears.

What happened? Did I swear again? It's so out of character. Must be something they put in the tea.

"She is a woman," I mused, when we'd stopped laughing, which was fair comment, in my experience of the weaker sex and anything mechanical, but put paid to any chances I had with Penny that afternoon. I've always thought that hotels have a peculiar erotic charge. It's that feeling of transience, I suppose, the separation from normal routine, the murmur of voices from other rooms. But Penny was a Saturday night sort of woman, and couldn't relax on anyone's sheets but her own. Frigid is a terrible word to use, especially about the dead. But is it any wonder I strayed? Instead, she came over all practical and insisted on a walk, to quieten the baby down and look for garages.

We found one just round the corner which had a repair shop, and a little further on a small Chinese restaurant where, later, we had dinner, me trying to eat with one hand while Flic sucked on my finger, a strange, toothless sensation one never forgets, like being fastened onto by a fish. Back at the pub we slept badly, woken constantly by crying. How deafening that sound is in the still, quiet pit of the night. I recall someone banging on one of our walls, or maybe even the floor above. Perhaps it was the landlady. Angrily, I banged back and shouted something, from a battle scene I think... Whoever it was didn't bother us again.

After breakfast we took the car to the garage, and a very friendly mechanic dropped what he was doing to carry out the repair. He had a way with babies as it happened. Flic subsided to an obedient cooing sound whenever he bent over her. Proper grease monkey, too. I nearly offered him a job.

We returned to the pub and paid the bill. The woman kept looking at the cot, when not scrutinising my cheque. She didn't exactly hold it up to the light, but otherwise gave me to think that I couldn't be trusted. Was that really the price we had agreed? How did I expect anyone to read my signature? Et cetera. Then, just as we were about to leave, she said:

"Did you find what you were looking for?"

"Oh, yes thanks," said Penny. "There's a garage round the corner. They were very helpful."

"A garage?" the woman said. She looked at us both as if we were mad. "Forgive me, what was it you were after again?"

"An exhaust system," Penny said.

The pencilled eyebrows vaulted, I can see them now, half way up her brow, like birds in the distance.

"Why, what did you think we wanted?" Penny glanced at me, appealing for help.

"I thought…," the woman began, halting for a moment and looking embarrassed. "I thought you said 'exorcist'."

I'm sorry, it still makes me roar. An exorcist! You couldn't make it up. And nor have I, by the way. I leave that sort of thing to those vipers in the press. What's more, Flic chose that moment to let out a positively inhuman wail and we all looked in her direction. If I'm honest, just for a moment, the idea didn't seem so absurd. It was the one explanation we hadn't considered.

"I'm *so* sorry," the woman said, "it's probably my hearing. Although," she turned to me, "to be honest, you do tend to mumble."

She was about the same age as my mother, too. The cow.

So there you have it, my little tale. Are those tears of laughter, my dear? I told you, the old magic is still there. I could have given you any number of tall stories from the theatre: Johnny this, Larry that. But you wanted something involving my daughter, and that's all I could come up with. Isn't that funny, something from 40 years ago, as fresh as if it were yesterday.

Do you know, I think I really must complain about that smell. It's getting worse. What do they think they're running here, some kind of bedpan motel?

Oh, must you leave? There's more tea in the pot, surely. Oh well, it's been nice. Sometimes people are a little in awe, but I don't sense that with you. No, I won't get up, if you don't mind. Someone will show you out. Mmm? One of the nurses? What on earth are they doing here?

There she goes, then. Goodbye, goodbye. A fine looking woman, for her age. Arse like a nectarine. What did they say she was called? Felicity I think. That's a beautiful name. I knew someone once...

Oh, no, don't leave! I've just remembered. What must you think of me, my dear? Felicity! Felicity!

What a pity. And just when it was coming back to me. The actor who stole my mumble – it was Marlon, wasn't it? Yes, I'm sure it was. Marlon something or other.

Fiona Joseph

Fiona Joseph is a graduate of the Diploma in Writing at Birmingham City University, where she won the National Academy of Writing Prize for Fiction. Her forthcoming book is *Beatrice: the Cadbury heiress who gave away her fortune*. Fiona is a member of Tindal Street Fiction Group, the Society of Authors and the Biographers' Club.

The Hills and the Fortune
by Fiona Joseph

The first time Con took Jas up the Lickeys a funny thing happened.

They were meeting around the corner from the Home, as soon as Jas could get away. The cow of a warden would only stamp her evening pass until half-nine and it was gone seven already. Jas snatched up the paper, crammed it in her jeans pocket and ran out the gate. Con was already leaning against the phone box.

'Hey, slow down, babe.' He put his arm around her waist and steered her towards Delphinium Lane because he wanted chips first and a go in the arcade.

The fish bar was at the bottom of the road, next door-but-one to the arcade where Con's mom worked as a cleaner. When Jas was still at school she used to see his mom most lunchtimes, polishing the gold-coloured window frames until they gleamed, or running a damp rag over the glass so you could see your reflection when walking past instead of all the jewellery and teddy bears laid out on their velvet beds. Funny to think all that was before she got together with Con. It felt like destiny.

'Want a scallop or something, angel?'

'Nah, it's alright.' What she couldn't say was that just the sight of him wrenched her appetite away and ripped all the clever words out of her brain. Sometimes she could only stand and stare at the gorgeousness of him — like some dumb special needs kid. In daylight his eyes were green with yellow around the edges, but when it got darker they turned brown.

Outside the fish bar she sat on the edge of a walled bed and watched Con go in. The view of his jeans hanging low around his arse as he leaned over the counter excited her. Something was gonna happen tonight. She ran her tongue around her mouth; it tasted fresh and minty still.

Con came out with two wooden forks between his teeth, a cone of chips and a can of Fanta. 'Want some?'

Jas shook her head again. He shrugged and began eating.

'So we going in the arcade?' she asked. To her, the arcade was a maze, edged with electronic monsters that flashed and squealed, like daleks. Con loved it though. He played one-armed, his other around her waist pulling her close and squeezing her hard whenever the machine coughed up its riches.

'Nah, I've got all my treasure right here, sweet.' He gently blew her fringe out of her eyes. 'I'll take you up the Lickeys later if you like.'

Then, the next moment, Adnan came round the corner on his purple bike and skidded to a halt in front of them. His Alsatian was leashed to the handlebar, slobber dripping from its jaws. You weren't supposed to ride a bike with a dog tied up like that. There should be laws or something to stop it. She watched as Con grinned and tipped the last of his chips onto the path; the dog hoovered them up in an instant.

Adnan was Con's mate from way back. He was thin, with a long head, and scooped-out flesh under his eyes and cheekbones. Looking at him made Jas think of cancer and white hospital sheets. He never smiled at her or said hi, just looked her up and down really slowly as if he was eyeing up one of the Mercs in Franklin Road.

'Yo bro, how's it going?' Adnan hooked his arm around Con's neck, pulling their heads together. 'Listen to this.' He put his headphone in Con's ear.

'Harsh, man,' Con said. They drifted towards the side alley. They had stuff to talk about. Always stuff.

Jas turned away and yanked at the daisies sprouting out of the grassy bed. She lined them up and pierced the stem of each one with her thumbnail creating a needle eye. She threaded one daisy through another until it was long enough to wrap around her wrist. The smell of weed, like rubber bands and burning rope, wafted over to her. As she glanced up she saw Adnan giving Con a stash of notes. Con took two notes off the pile, gave them back to Adnan, and he pocketed the rest.

Adnan lobbed her a vicious look and she ripped the chain off her wrist. Now he was showing Con something on his phone. 'Look, we gotta do it, man, we're losing market share.'

The sun was fading and Jas stroked the crop of goosebumps on her arms. If Con didn't get a move on, the evening would slip away to nothing. She remembered the time when she'd got back to the Home twenty minutes late and the warden bitches had gone nuclear. Curfewed her for six whole weeks. No way was she risking that again, not now she had Con.

Then finally he said goodbye to Adnan and came over, 'Okay, hon?'

The sky was pretty as they walked up to the hills; all streaked with peach and lemon puffs. Awesome colours for a top or maybe a dress one day, when she had a job and some money. Her feet slipped around inside her sandals. Even they were cast-offs, worn by fuck knows how many people.

She grabbed at the berries from a nearby bush.

'Sorry about just now,' Con said.

'Can we eat these?'

'I'd like to eat you,' he answered, and took a blackberry from her, biting into it and rubbing it across her bottom lip. She waited with her hands by her sides while he held her chin and kissed off the juice.

They climbed to the top of a grassy slope, so high up you could see across the whole city. She felt the vastness of everything around her. She and Con were an island surrounded by shimmering sea below: the furnace chimneys, each one a lighthouse, and the motorway, a twinkling pier that stretched out towards the skyline. Traffic whispered from a faraway shore.

'Imagine if all this was ours,' Con said. 'Our kingdom. I'd make you my queen, my street-cred princess.' He tapped his front trouser pocket: 'I've got some, y'know, thingies on me.' And then he kissed her, the corners of his mouth tasting all salty and his tongue still warm from the chips. He put his jacket underneath them and then got right on top of her. He kept most of his weight on his elbows so that it was only his hips she felt sliding against hers. Her hand travelled the nape of his neck where his cropped hair felt like velvet beneath her fingertips. She closed her eyes. Waited for something to happen.

'Undo my belt,' he said, but before she could he cried out, 'Shit man!' He rolled off and curled into a ball away from her.

She stared at his rocking back. What had she done? She leaned over him and saw a child's face, all screwed up with pain and fury.

'I've come in my pants,' he said. 'Bollocking hell.' Then he laughed and everything felt okay again. He acted like he was so grown-up but really he was more of a kid than she was. He was still smiling about it when he took her back to the Home, just after nine. Outside the phonebox he checked her over, picking a bud out of her hair and wiping a smudge off her cheek with his thumb.

He took her left hand and kissed it. She forced herself not to pull it away. It was the hand one of the foster dads had pressed against the electric fire, when she'd been slow to learn. The scars were raised pink stripes across her palm. Maybe they weren't too bad because Con never said anything. One day she'd tell him about it but not yet.

He pressed the flat of her hand against his jeans. She could feel the outline of him underneath the damp cold denim.

'See that's you, babe —that's what you done to me.'

Jas liked hearing him say that. It made her shiver and feel warm at the same time.

'And next time, it'll be better 'cos I'm gonna make you come,'

Con said, with a half-smile. He held her face between his hands, trapping her gaze. 'You know, come; c-u-m.'

Jas twisted her head away. A chip wrapper scooted across the road, before hugging the lamppost.

His phone burst into rap and he stared at the screen.

'Sorry hon, I gotta go.' He began walking backwards, saying, 'See you next week.' The abruptness of it knifed her in the stomach, and she turned to go inside. 'Hey, angel!' he called. 'Sleep tight. Love ya!' Then he was gone.

Next time they met, a week later, he hadn't forgotten his promise. 'I'll make it good for you,' he whispered into her ear. Questions swarmed like gnats inside her head, never stopping long enough for her to work out the answers. She wasn't sure what was actually going to happen to her, or what she had to do to make it happen. Whether or not he had to put it inside.

'Not here,' he said. 'We'll go up the Lickeys again.' He told her she had a surprise waiting for her. And she could see in his walk, the way he jigged along, that he was wired with enough excitement for both of them.

They went through the car park, past the kids' play area at the bottom of the hills, and squeezed through a wire fence. He led her to a wood, where the trees were so thick that they only let little bits of light through, making patterns on the ground. Low bushes scratched at her jeans, and she felt crumbs of dirt work their way into her sandals.

He told her to close her eyes, they were nearly there.

'You can open them now.' She saw a fallen tree with a red blanket thrown over its trunk, and loads of cushions on the ground next to it. As she moved closer she saw another blanket made of fur spread out on the ground. Near the edge of it there were two glasses and a bottle of pop. No, cider. Her mouth felt dry. In a metal bin a fire had been burning and she could see the red and white glow of an upright log inside.

'You done all this? How d'you do it?'

'It's totally private. Our own little kingdom.'

Then he scooped her up like a baby and spun her round so that she shrieked for him to stop. But he carried on and she gave into it. To think he'd done all this, just for her! She fell out of his arms, all drunk and laughing with dizziness and love.

As she steadied herself she caught sight of something on the ground on the other side of the clearing: purple metal. She squinted. A wheel came into focus.

'Is that Adnan's bike?'

'What?'

'Over there.' She stepped forward to look but Con was holding her arm.

'He helped me get stuff ready. You know, the way mates do and all that. No big deal.'

'But he don't like me. Where is he?'

'He's fucked off, okay? It's not like he's gonna stay and watch.' It was the first time she'd heard Con laugh like that, like she was special needs after all.

He tried to pull her close but this time she wriggled away.

'What is it, for fuck's sake?'

'I don't know, it just feels... different.' Spoiled, she wanted to say. She looked up to the ceiling of trees. 'It's like someone's watching.'

Con sat on the tree trunk, on the red blanket.

'But you know, it wouldn't be that bad if you think about it. Adnan could take some pictures if we let him. I've got this mate, right. He takes videos and stuff of his girlfriend on his phone, nothing cheap, only classy stuff, and you can sell them to this bloke and make a packet.'

'Stop it.'

He grabbed her wrists and pulled her onto her knees in front of him.

'Don't you know, you're sitting on a goldmine?' His eyes were all shining now, like when he hit the jackpot in the arcade, like he was seeing a fountain of tumbling coins.

She looked at the ground around her. So this was the surprise. He'd got money hidden, buried right underneath her maybe. That's why he'd brought her here.

Con sighed. 'You don't get it, do you? I mean every bitch is sitting on a fortune.'

It took a few moments for her to work it out, but this time the answer, the knowledge, came to her in a slow and careful understanding. And while the blocks of comprehension were fixing themselves together, and stacking themselves up, she felt a spark ignite inside. In her mind she started to run back out of the clearing, away from him and from the flame that was trailing her.

But it was too late. She flew at him with her fists. 'I hate you. I fucking hate you.' She wanted to take his hand and stick it in the fire.

And so she made herself run from him, out of the wood and to the top of the hill where she knelt and screamed until she was spent. Just behind her she felt a breeze and in her mind she saw ashes blowing over the hills, over her, and down onto the kingdom below.

Derek Littlewood

Derek Littlewood teaches literature in The School of English, Birmingham City University. He attended an Arvon writing course with David Morley and Alison MacLeod and subsequently poetry workshops with George Szirtes and Esther Morgan at The Poetry School. *The Sunken Gardens* was written as a response to the photography of Paul O' Donnell of Birmingham Institute of Art and Design.

The Sunken Gardens
by Derek Littlewood

for Paul O'Donnell

Darkling

> *The Sunken Garden*
> *All her sorrows, bitter rue.*
> *Breathe not, trespass not,*
> *of this green and darkling spot.*
>   *de la Mare*

Argentum

> *Sleep among the midst of lots.*
You should be as the wings of a dove
feathered in silver...
My dove in the hollow places of the wall,
show me your face. Open to me, my love,
my dove, my undefiled - for my head
is full of spirits, my hair of the dregs of the night.

Columba

Framing the scene in camera as one fluidity; middle,
then seeking a left,
before searching for a right - together- a triptych of darkness.
Slats with an effusion of buddleia in Camden,
    a locked door with peeled render,
above scatterings of broken glass,
    flies a fluttering dove
towards a dark wound. Smoke or oil sheened
on a wall, scarred with a horizontal slit.
    Here, Irish Mary did her trick for a tenner
    while thinking of Doolin, thinking of nothing.

As a dog is drawn to its vomit, so are we
pulled between Rugby and Stoke;
pain don't work, sprayed on a wall
in attempted refutation the plaster gouged with a screwdriver,
paint mazed over brick.
    Here, Davey downed the last of the warming rum,
    then hawked a gob of phlegm ruefully.

Mojo

Between two ventilation shafts in Manchester,
there's a doss, where you can lie against the cold;
to the right a shop window filmed with filthy gauze,
a bandaged wound leaking pus, concealing
the interior with grey dust.
>Here, while her man was away, Anna took heroin orally
>and was as sick as a dog

up against the wall. All the secretions of the body tremble
  with danger,
sweat, shit, piss, sputum, vomit, spunk and bloody flux
  smeared over a window
    in abjection, negation, rejection of self. Foul, except for tears.

Lacrimae rerum

Tears water the weeds in wild places.
They flower profusely through the wastes.

cleavers, nettles, bindweed
ragwort, henbane, scurvy-grass
dogrose, willow herb, plantain
hogweed, balsam, heartsease
yarrow, nightshade, comfrey

Woe to the provoking and redeemed city,
the dove.

Between dark and dark, an infinite tonality of grays,
between my fingers slip the weeds. Dodging and burning.

Spite of despondence, of the inhuman dearth
of noble natures, of the gloomy days,
of all the unhealthy and o'er-darkened days,
made for our searching: yes, in spite of all,
some shape of beauty moves away the pall
from our dark spirits.

I am the crunch of littered glass.
I am the stench of fetid air.
I am the missing tread on the stair.

I am fire.
I am ice.
I am the enchanter's silken voice.

I am wind.
I am rain.
I am the expression of pain.

Kate Mascarenhas

Kate Mascarenhas is a PhD student of Children's Literature. Her publication credits include film reviews, poetry and academic articles about *Doctor Who*. In 2010 she co-edited the National Academy of Writing's third anthology. She is currently drafting a fantasy novel set in the Anchor Exchange, Birmingham's hidden network of underground tunnels.

The Boy from Chalk Street
by Kate Mascarenhas

The workmen in the garden start packing before twilight. Through the bedroom window I overhear the old builder, Lennox, say he is taking the van to the tip; he tells the boy builder to stay behind and hose down the slabs. He'll see him, Lennox says, in the morning.

At this time of year, I would normally be marking mock exams, keen to finish before Christmas. Instead I am knitting winter woollens and making jam - bland pursuits that my son, Jack, thinks are appropriate to an aging widow. I took early retirement in the spring. The plan was to emigrate: prepare the house for market, and sell up. But there was more to rectify than I realised. Each new discovery of decay or shoddy workmanship keeps me here in limbo a little longer.

Limbo is just where Jack likes me. Not that he's averse to the improvements. He's shrewd. If my house is well-kept it means more money for him, in the long run. Provided I don't fritter any proceeds on foreign travel. He even obtained a few building quotes on my behalf - a simple enough matter, because his chief income is from letting property. Since the renovations began, he has driven from Hereford once a week to interrogate the workmen. Today he castigated me for taking Lennox tea.

'Don't get too friendly,' he said. 'Lennox will take advantage. And don't let the boy in either. They'll both pilfer, given the chance.'

If I admit something has already gone missing, he'll gloat. A silver-framed photo has disappeared from above the fire – the picture of Rory, my old red Labrador. I convince myself there's no need to give Jack the satisfaction. Things quite regularly fall down the back of the mantelpiece.

This evening I stand at the window of Jack's old bedroom, and watch Lennox depart by the back gate. The only sound now is the *shush-shush* of a broom. I turn my attention to Lennox's apprentice; the boy builder, still in his teens. At first I think he is sweeping pools of water towards the drain. Soon I realise he is arranging damp brick dust into a picture – I can't tell what of, from here. His movements are swift. He looks at his handiwork, paces in a circle, and finally stops. Finished.

Down the patio steps he strides.

He loses his footing. *Thwack*! Yet he does not cry out. He lies motionless.

For a moment I am still too. When he fails to stir, I turn and run, down the stairs, through the kitchen and outside.

I shiver. No coat.

'Are you all right?' I ask.

He sits up. Sweat shines on his forehead.

'I'm not sure. My ankle.'

I sit next to him.

'Do you mind if I take a look? I have some first aid training.'

He nods, wincing, towards his left foot. I lift the muddied trouser hem. There's no sign of a break.

'You've sprained it, I think. Can you walk?'

He looks uncertain.

'I'll give you a hand,' I say.

I reach under his arm, so he can lean on me. A smell of sawdust and sweat and tobacco exudes from him. There's an incongruous note of vanilla, too. His ribcage feels as ridged as a xylophone. My thoughts turn to Jack; he was never this slight. He was sturdy and red-faced right through childhood, like a middle-aged landlord in miniature.

The boy takes a step without complaining, but inhales through his teeth. I make a decision.

'Come inside and sit down. You can call the doctor's from there.'

He nods, his jaw still gritted with discomfort.

Once indoors I get him comfortable. I fetch him the pouffe to keep his leg elevated; a pack of peas; a cup of tea. Two elderly co-codamol. With a pop the gas fire emits its purple heat. A batch of marmalade is simmering on the stove. My own cup of tea is on the table.

'The doctor's surgery will be closed,' he mutters.

'There's nobody else you want to ring?'

'When I've finished my drink I'll call Lennox. He can drive me home.'

'What's your name?'

I expect him to say *Lee* or *Dan*.

'Dovekie.'

'Not really?' I laugh. 'Like the custard?'

At the back of the larder I still have some Dovekie's Custard; I wonder if it goes off. The powder used to be sold in red tins with a parrot on the label. I hadn't made custard in years. But every Physics teacher, at one time, told their pupils how Dovekie Factory exploded. Their premises went up in flames because uncovered powder mixed with the air.

The boy looks clammy. He needs distraction till the painkillers work.

'Is Dovekie a nickname?'

He shakes his head. I stir a spoon of sugar into my tea.

'You're not some kind of custard-powder magnate, are you?' I joke.

He doesn't smile.

'Those Dovekies are dead,' he says. 'They died in the fire.'

His terseness makes me uneasy. It seems impossible that only a few moments before, I could confuse him with the boys at my school. There are trenches in his brow and hollows in his cheeks. The indigo glow from the gas elements ages him. He might be a century old.

Just who, I wonder, *have I let in*?

'Before the explosion,' he begins, 'there were one hundred and forty four houses on a road called Popinjay Lane ...'

The terraces once formed a terracotta border round Dovekie's Factory. Afterwards the street resembled a chain of dominoes. There was only one house still whole at the end.

Those who escaped were homeless. Any surviving orphans were taken into care. Kelly, who had lived all her twelve years in the single house that remained, roamed through the rubble by herself. Her mother had been on the gin long before the explosion. There was no question of moving away now.

Dovekie's was gutted. To Kelly, the factory's East side looked like an open doll's house: intact but exposed to the air. Girders protruded from the remaining walls into what had been the West half of the building. But what really interested Kelly were the chalk drawings. What kept her piecing through the ruins, with her grey-haired mongrel Sam, were the dense pictures in yellow chalk that spidered over the factory walls. They were drawn each night. A pattern of birds, repeated one after the other. After every rainfall they were redrawn. The pictures were appropriate, because birds seemed to be the only living things left on Popinjay Lane. Not that it was known by that name for much longer. Across the city people began to talk, fearfully, of Chalk Street. It was a place that no one wanted to go.

Eventually Kelly discovered the artist. It was a summer morning, and her routine was the same as usual. She stood, in her school uniform, before the front window, while her mother combed her hair.

'Keep still,' her mother said.

These ponytails always gave Kelly headaches, because they were scraped too tightly from her face. It was pointless to complain. Her mother was always gruff in the morning, and drunk by the afternoon. Kelly focused on the view from the window while her mother twisted a cherry bobble round and round so many times Kelly thought it would snap. Above the peeling white paint of the ledge, the East side of the factory filled the frame. The red brick wall was cut diagonally with the zig-zag of an iron fire escape – and around that, the yellow birds snaked upwards between the mortar.

'Don't go lingering in the street again.' The last hairband was in place. 'Wouldn't want a ruddy great brick to fall on your head, now, would we?'

Kelly didn't reply. She knelt to secure a lead on Sam's collar. Above the leather strip were six pearlescent spots of scar tissue. Cigarette burns that Kelly had watched the older kids brand in his flesh. They were dead kids, now. Sam closed his amber eyes and whimpered. Tail down, he led the way to the door.

It was too hot outdoors for a school jumper. Kelly wrapped the sleeves round her waist. As soon as she felt sure her mother had retreated, she made her way into the factory. It was there she saw the boy; he was about her own age, crouched among the rubble on the ground floor. Sam strained at the lead, tail wagging, and gave one short, happy, yap.

'S'nice dog,' the boy said, as she approached. He looked wistful. 'I'd like a dog.'

Kelly frowned. She recognised this boy. He had been Mr Dovekie's son, and his name was Luke.

'I thought you'd moved to that big home, with the others,' she said. The other orphans, she meant. He shrugged.

'I don't know where the others went. I go to a different school now.'

You've bunked off today, Kelly thought. He'd been bullied when he went to her school, she knew that. Bullied by the kids, and bullied when he went home. They all knew Mr Dovekie beat him with the business end of a power lead. She supposed that should make her sympathetic. But life didn't always work that way. He didn't help himself. Like looking so pleased to see the dog. He looked that way at people too. So eager to please. It made you want to kick him.

'You did these drawings?' she said.

He nodded.

'You like birds,' she said.

'Are they... are they any good?'

'They're OK,' she said begrudgingly, as though she had not gone looking for him. 'Why birds though?'

He looked away.

'There are other drawings inside. I like to imagine that the things in my pictures belong to me.' He paused. 'Mostly birds are less dangerous. That's why they're on the outside walls.'

'What do you mean?'

He ruffled the top of Sam's head and smiled.

'I use magic chalk,' he said.

'Magic chalk! And you're a magician, I suppose. D'you think I'm stupid?'

'No.'

'Well *you* must be stupid then.'

'I can prove it's true.'

'How?'

'Didn't you have another pet?'

'A cat,' she said. 'Polly.'

'I remember.' He turned to the nearest wall, and found a blank patch.

'She was a tabby,' Kelly added.

'I remember,' he repeated quietly, while sketching an outline. After a few minutes the chalk was worn to a nub. The boy knelt and dragged his hand through the sandy earth at his feet. With his thumb he rubbed soil along the cat's yellow stripes, until the colour was right.

'There,' he announced. It was really very good, Kelly knew.

'What's so magic about *that*?' she asked.

'When you go to bed tonight,' he said, 'she'll be on your pillow.'

'It's only a picture.'

'If I'm right, then you owe me.'

'You are crackers.'

'It's not fair you should have two pets,' he replied. 'And your dog likes me. If Polly comes back, tonight, like I say, then you should give me your dog. That's only fair.'

'Yeah,' Kelly said, her voice heavy with sarcasm. 'You can have my dog.'

'Good,' he said.

Kelly knew, deep down, that she should have told him clearly: of course you can't have him, my dog belongs to me. But she let the boy misunderstand her, knowing he misunderstood so many people, so much of the time, and that was why he was picked on. He drew attention to himself, with his stupid smiling face and his talk of 'magic chalk.'

When she got back that night, it was nearly ten. She always stayed outside for as long as possible to avoid her mother. In the days before the explosion, Mrs Reddish at number seventeen would see her playing outdoors, and call her in for a decent dinner. She remembered how gratefully she had eaten; and how little difference missing meals made now.

Her mother was splayed on the sofa. The empty bottle was on the floor, just like every night. Kelly took off her shoes and crept upstairs.

Her school uniform was full of ash. Drifts blew all day over the burnt out street. She brushed the cinders from her top, allowing them to fall on the landing carpet. A piece or two coasted before her and settled on the bedroom door knob. The handle turned of its own accord.

And Kelly, seeing what was in the room, screamed.

'What! What!' her mother shouted, roused by the noise.

Kelly froze. Not at her mother's voice, but because of the *thing* on the bed.

Lying on her pillow was an animal she recognised, but

knew could not be hers. Compelled to look closer, even in her revulsion, Kelly tip-toed over the rug. The creature mewed and began licking its brown fur. There was a circular name tag swinging from its collar. Kelly glimpsed her own handwriting on the insert.

Nausea surged in her gullet.

The cat stood, padded over the candlewick and leapt onto her shoulder. Then Kelly *was* sick, all over the carpet; because a year before, Kelly had watched her cat die. She had watched Polly run yowling, aflame, with the smell of cooking meat in her wake.

Kelly did not sleep that night, despite throwing the cat from the window. Other memories from the explosion had been disturbed. In the morning she intended to seek the boy out and make him pay.

The summer nights were short, and she rose at five. She fastened her shoes, but did not change from her nightgown, because her uniform was streaked with vomit. Though she knew the boy would not arrive for hours, if at all that day, she intended to wait for him in the factory.

The sun was low in the sky. She ascended the fire escape to the third floor. Blackened office furniture was still inside. Maybe, she thought, this was where Dovekie had made his big decisions. She curled up in a charred seat, and looked out at the ruined landscape. I'm the doll, she thought, when the front of the house is off. Her eye travelled up the grey streak of road no one took anymore. In the distance, tall office blocks, like needles bristling from a pin cushion, marked the centre of the city.

From here, she would see the boy coming.

As the sun reached the top of the furthest sky scraper, she caught sight of the boy turning into Chalk Street. She walked to the precipice of the building, so that he might see her, too, as he grew closer.

He waved at her delightedly.

'Hi! Hi! I was right, wasn't I?' he called. 'Did you bring your dog?'

'Yes,' she lied. 'He's right here, waiting for you.'

When he reached the East side she had a bird's eye view of his head before he disappeared into the rooms below. She could hear his footfall on the last flight of steps before the door burst open.

'Why on earth did you come up here?' he said, laughing. He looked around, searching for the dog. His expression grew confused. The sun caught the brown of his irises. For a moment they looked amber. *Like Sam's*, Kelly thought.

'I wanted to show you the view,' she said. 'Haven't you been up here?

He nodded, uncertainly.

'Of course. It was my family's factory.'

'But not since it's had this wonderful view.'

'Where's your dog?'

'Oh, he's somewhere about. Come forward and look for him. You'll be able to see him from here.'

'No,' he said, unsure. 'I don't think I will.'

'Why?'

'I think you might be angry with me,' he cried; and he ran away.

'Come back,' she shouted, unable to keep the rage from her voice. She gave chase. If she had to run him off the edge of the second floor, she would do it.

But he was fast, and he had a head start. She didn't catch him on the second floor, or the first. When she reached the ground he was already drawing rapidly across the brickwork.

'What are you doing?' she shrieked. 'Making more filthy dead things?'

His face was wet with tears.

'You promised I could have your dog,' he said, his hand darting over the wall. She looked again at what he was drawing. Long lines, and ovals. Snake like shapes. The chalk was mingling with the brick dust, and the grime and the ash, to make black and orange and yellow and red. *Flames*.

A stray piece of ash aggravated her throat. She coughed.

'What are you doing?' she repeated. At her words, another drift of ash caught the current. Cinders filled her eyes and mouth.

Before she could see again she heard the first screams. People crying and the whine of sirens. Coughing overwhelmed her. Racked her; choked her.

Staggering away from the boy, she looked at the ground. The chalk and the soot ran in smoking rivulets of water. There were firemen everywhere, but it was already too late. The explosion had caught the trees on the West side. In minutes the houses were up in flames. People were fleeing from their doorways like lice from rotten wood. Kelly watched Mrs Reddish run from number seventeen with her baby in a blanket. But there was nowhere to go. The fire was everywhere. Kelly's own mother was wailing and shouting, and she collapsed in the street: Kelly knew this was not because of the gin, but the smoke in her lungs.

Through the smoke Kelly fought her way home. The front door was open. With her arms outstretched she reached the stairs. The fire never travelled this far, she knew; theirs was the only intact house on the road. She crawled along the landing floor, where the air was cleanest, until she arrived at the bedroom.

A girl with a cherry bobble in her hair was lying on the candlewick. Her mouth was streaked black, and her eyes stared at the ceiling, unblinking. At her feet lay a grey-haired dog. Dead.

Kelly fell back to the floor, gasping. Somewhere, in one of the inner factory walls, she knew there was a chalk drawing she had not seen. One of her, and Sam, and her mother. Perhaps it even included the house. How many other families had the boy drawn, looking for something he couldn't find? A hundred and forty-three? Maybe Sam was what he'd wanted all the time. *Animals were safer*, she remembered. No beatings; no bullying. No drinking, come to that.

She knew why he hadn't raised his parents. Some deaths were a blessing.

'The flames stopped with the next rainfall,' Dovekie says. 'And the boy didn't go back again.'

He leans back in the arm chair, and I wonder if he is still in pain. No; the co-codamol is doing its job. I watch him fall asleep. His features are illuminated more warmly than before. The gas elements have turned from indigo to coral.

While he sleeps I test the marmalade, but it is still too soft to set. Once more I am restless. I find myself staring at him. In slumber he looks like a boy again.

There is a woollen throw on the sideboard, newly crocheted with primrose yarn. He sighs as I drape it over his legs.

I try to remember what Jack looked like as a sleeping child. It is hard to acknowledge how little tenderness I felt towards him. When he was born I half believed he was a changeling. A stranger, with nothing of me in him at all. I allow myself to daydream. This boy offers another chance. He can sleep in Jack's old room, and he will need me – as my school boys did. I won't leave for Spain.

The urge to brush the fringe from his forehead is irresistible. I tuck the edges of the blanket round him. So absorbed am I, that the sound of an animal, scratching and whining at the back door, quite startles me.

The noise stops as soon as my hand touches the handle. Once outside I switch on the patio light. No one is there.

For the second time this evening, I shiver. The brick dust picture is still on the paving slabs. I failed to notice it, while I was helping Dovekie. He has drawn the outline of a dog.

Not Sam; this is no grey mongrel. More like a Labrador.

Looking around, I half expect to see the flash of Rory's russet fur amongst the ferns. I touch the red grains on the concrete, unsure what I hope to find. Some trace of yellow chalk, maybe.

I turn back towards the house. What was it Kelly had asked – *how many other families*?

'You can stop looking,' I will tell Luke Dovekie. I will go inside, and prepare his new room, and then at last I'll wake him with the news he can stay. His eyes will open. They will shine like the oranges bubbling in the pot.

Roy McFarlane

Roy was born in Birmingham of Jamaican parentage. He's had poems published in anthologies and in magazines such as *Under the Radar* and he's been resident poet for Starbucks. He's presently Birmingham Poet Laureate 2010/11 and in his busy schedule he's working on his first novel *Somebody's Daughter*.

We don't have to carry our Fathers
by Roy McFarlane

I found my father's love letters

I found my father's love letters
in strange and obscure places,
hidden in dark secret spaces,
where memories had closed the doors.

I found blank letters, with matching cards and envelopes.
A small drawer filled with letters unfinished,
crossed through, curling at the edges,
turning in the colour of time.

There was one in Marquez's *Love in a time of Cholera*
sandwiched somewhere between
Fermina's rejection of Floretina
and a lifetime of loving, waiting for true love.

I found some penned in a note pad, half-written, half-thought,
scribbled to capture fleeting thoughts,
earnest in writing the emotional overflow
that time edits into streams flowing over with love.

I found one folded
lost in the attic
an elegy to love
that time had forgotten.

I searched to find the true name to those letters entitled *my love*.
A secret lover? Distant lover? First time lover?
or even my mother of whom you gave a thousand names
but I never heard you call her *my love*.

I wonder if they ever received their letters,
an amended version, a completed version
refined and acceptable, filled with rose petals,
signed and sealed with your love.

Dreams of rivers

The old man dreams of rivers
Where young men are swimming
Cooking *boyo*,
Drinking *mannish water* under
Banana trees swaying
In a Caribbean breeze.
Now he's rubbing knees
On a cold winter morning
Looking through
Frost pane windows;
Reflecting on younger days
As a newly wed
Bedding and working the soil
That enriched your soul
A plot of land,
With orange and mango trees
And a ground filled
With cassava, coco and yam
And a mule name Betty.
Now he works for British steel
A soulless, thankless task
Where his hands are blackened
By the dirt of industry
Where chains swing from steel girders
Carrying their bounty,
Across molten rivers
Forged from the fire of the foundry.
The old man dreams of rivers
Standing in his long johns and *mariner*
Looking through his many suits
Leaving his family blissfully asleep.

Notes;

"Boyo": Also known as Blue Drawers and Dukunu is a sweet cornmeal dumpling/pudding which was wrapped in banana leaves and boiled.

"Mannish water": A Jamaican cuisine known as goat soup, made up of various goat parts, seasoned with herbs and spices, and cooked along with vegetables and food.

"Mariner": A man's undershirt, tank-top style of vest.

The weight lays heavy on his shoulders

They're telling lies
He announced with eloquence
A descendant of Jewish migrant
It's a lie any notion that the Dutch
Are a tolerant nation.

The weight of the holocaust
Lay heavy on his shoulder
As he stands there and wavers
He stands firm in the knowledge
Of the Dutch involvement in slavery
And the spice trades that made them
The richest country in Europe.

They're telling lies he announced
In between red wine and other drinks
Pouring and flowing
With the atrocities
And the complacency of a city
And the stories of migration
That has been written out of history.

He's telling lies Geert Wilders
Head of a popular party
The right wing bastard
Comparing the Koran
To Hitler's Mein Kempf
And Islam to a backward religion
He's no different to Goebbels.

So this Dutch native of Harlem
In sober moments will write another book
And he'll write these lies
Eloquently through poetry
On behalf of his fathers and forefathers
He's tongue liberated
By the liberal intake from the grape vine
Speaking freely of the suffering
Of a persecuted generation
They're still telling lies, telling lies
They're still telling lies.

We no longer carry our fathers

Mustafa has carried his father
In so many ways in dreams
As I have carried mine across streams of words
Fathers who grew strong by rivers
Crossed oceans in their strength
Are now buried far from their father's lands.

We seem to share this affinity
As thou we were mirrored.
At their feet we learned so many things
And now we know our hallelujahs and inshallas
Quote chapters and surahs
And share Christ in our conversations.

We know the meaning of love lost
And being caught adrift
As though we had killed an albatross.

He's Moroccan
And I'm of the Caribbean
City Laureates in different cities
Our identities are fluid but we
Know the source from which it came.

And we hold our bellies and laugh
At our words caught up
In the mainstream of white society
Lost on the banks of mistranslation
Words written, re-written to be better digested.

But we hold our fathers dear
For they have written us into existence
Fathers who have already showed us the way
And we hear our ancestors say
That we no longer after carry the
Burdens of our forefathers
We just need to walk side by side
With them along the way.

Geoff Mills

Geoff Mills recently moved back to north London where he acts, writes, teaches, tells jokes and sells. In his spare time he guzzles lager and feasts on cake. His one-man comedy show Bag of Nuts will be seen and instantly admired in a number of venues very soon.

Love and Loss
by Geoff Mills

A Day at the Beach

And so up and up and up we went, the air thinning our breath thickening. Our twenty-fifth, our Silver Anniversary. Her hair was a little silver now, her walk a little slower, her form a little fuller, her speech a little heavier. But still she was she, her, the one I wanted, the one I married – and yes, still. Still. The one I loved.

The wind bit, snapped at our faces, sky sea spaces opening up before us: sometime bliss, grey abyss. I reached my arm around her duffled shoulders, pressed my lips against her silk thin cheek a smile. A kind of smile. A trying to be smile, but not quite being. We edged closer, closer now, terrain behind, soupy emptiness ahead. And then. And then she was gone. Lurched forward, dropped plumb line, swallowed up - feet first - by the mists. A dull thud - maybe a crack, or a smack, reporting her arrival – her departure. I heard the seagulls squeal their insane soliloquies, to the rush and roil of the shoreline, sensed a seismic shift within. Screaming seconds scoured my world. And who now, I begged the weeping clouds, will hold me as I sleep?

Echoes

I felt your smooth skin press against the length of me, and your breath burn my face. You were there for only a second. You disappeared before I could respond. That brief charge of heat has passed through chill days since.

You came to me again, on the bus as I went to work. My cheek was resting against the cold glass, the rain's insistent patter hypnotizing, and the humming vibrations of the bus rocking me into dull oblivion. You sidled up and brushed a hand through my hair, an electric thrill tickling my skull. You whispered soothing susurrations, caressing the hollow of my ear, echoing with a meaning I could not grasp. I have replayed it again and again, sought its heat against the bare backdrop of my days.

And more days I waited, days cold and interminable: your echoes resounding around a life scooped empty.

Today I saw your face. I was at the supermarket. I stood at the till staring towards the aisles and took you as another customer, but then you turned and looked straight at me. You wore a smile I could not read. What was it exactly? I was staring at you long after you had disappeared, the cashier calling out at me, to bring me back to her world. She asked me if I was ok. Yes of course, I said.

Yes. Of course.

I've been feeling strange lately; things have been jolted out of place. The world I inhabit now seems more like a sickly projection. These days I go through the motions, follow a script I must have written in my saner days. But what would it matter, if, on the tube, I were to take my clothes off, start gnawing on the ear of the man sat next to me, tell my boss to go screw his fat face? Sometimes I think I will do these things to see if it will, to smash through the numbness of my life.

Tonight you came and stayed a while. I was staring at the television when you came into the room and sat down beside me. I had been expecting you. We did not speak, I did not even look at you, but you placed your arm behind my head and I sank onto your chest. You stroked my hair. You did not tell me, but I knew this would be the last time. I understood you perfectly. You'd decided that I had better go it alone, that these febrile visitations were doing me no good. You're right of course. Sever and progress, cut lose and float free - leave me with only the echoes of that other life by which to remember you. I see then, if that is how it must be. Tonight I shall sleep alone.

Tammy Palmer

Tammy Palmer has written, produced and directed a number of short films, which have been produced by her independent film company. Her short films have been screened at various events across the country. *The Aftershock* is the first part of her first radio drama, written in response to the Haiti earthquake of 2010, for which she is currently seeking a producer. She lives in Birmingham with her fiancé and their 9-year-old son.

The Aftershock
by Tammy Palmer

SCENE 1.
RADIO NEWS REPORTER/NEWSROOM

REPORTER: A massive 7.0-magnitude earthquake has struck the Caribbean nation of Haiti.
The extent of the devastation is still unclear but there are fears thousands of people may have died.
Haiti's worst quake in two centuries hit south of the capital Port-au-Prince on Tuesday, wrecking the presidential palace, UN HQ and other government buildings.
Many people have spent the night outside amid fears of aftershocks.
The Red Cross say up to three million people have been affected.
Describing the earthquake as a "catastrophe", Haiti's envoy to the US said the cost of the damage could run into billions.
A number of nations, including the US, UK and Venezuela are gearing up to send aid...

FADE OUT

SCENE 2.
UNDER THE MINISTRY OF FINANCE/ UNDER THE RUBBLE

FADE UP

FX DUST FALLING

PATRICK: **Cough, cough. Arrrrggggghhhhhh**

FX PANTING AND HEAVY BREATHING

PATRICK: **Jesus. What…where…**

I am trapped, beneath concrete, beneath the building.
I am surrounded by darkness and dust.
I stay still, too scared to move.

But I'm alive. I'm breathing. I'm conscious.

But my legs, it's my thighs; they are held down by something. Stuck in place. But I can move my toes.
The back of my head, which lies on concrete, feels wet and cold.
I am holding something in my left hand but my left arm is trapped and I can't see or feel exactly what it is. I can't remember what it is but I hold on to it..

I try to sit up, but it's impossible.

PATRICK: **Arrrrgggghhhhh.**

I am pinned down.

I can hear sound but I'm not sure what it is.

FX FAINT SOUND OF A SIREN

A bolt of red-hot pain shoots up my legs.

PATRICK: **Arrgggggg. Holy Lord.**

I try to think clearly but the pain engulfs my thoughts, smothering them to obliteration. I feel nauseas, dizzy and pass out, falling into the unconsciousness of nothingness.

SCENE 3.
IN THE STREET/CARREFOUR, HAITI

FADE UP

FX MUSIC (VOODOO DRUMS) AND THE SOUND OF THE STREET

PATRICK: I am falling, falling, falling, I've fallen...

I am dreaming.
My mother is calling to me:

PATRICIA: **Patrick, Patrick.**

She is running toward me, crying. She grabs me; her black hands pitch dark on the sleeves of my luminous white shirt. She hugs me. She chants my name:

PATRICIA: (Whimpering)
Patrick, Patrick, Patrick.

SCENE 4
UNDER THE MINISTRY OF FINANCE/
UNDER THE RUBBLE

PATRICK: Wake, waking, I wake. I'm awake.

I come to, not knowing how long I have been unconscious.

The pain had subsided a little but now panic rises up from the pit of my stomach up into my throat.
Was I going to die, here – alone?

PATRICK: **Am I going to die here…alone?**

Hello. Is anybody there?

O' dear Lord, I don't want to die.
I had done something terrible – unforgivable.
Is this my judgement?

Some time earlier, in this very room, I was stood facing him, then, then something happened.
I was standing in this room and I was on the ground – feet flat on the floor one minute and the next, I was above it. My feet wouldn't fall where I placed them. The ground was moving beneath me. The furniture slid and jumped around and under me.
Then, seconds after, the building collapsed.

How? Why?
A bomb, anti-government protesters, a gang or my brother!

FX FAINT SOUND OF HELICOPTER

A rescue team must be above, looking for me and other staff.
They will know people are in here; officials, staff, dining room attendants, gardeners, cleaners, me; we are all in here.
People I have met here at the Finance Ministry, all the good people will be trapped too.

Carel. Beautiful Carel in the clerical office.

PATRICK: **Carel**
Carel

Carel can't hear me and if she can she may not be able to answer.

(Shouting)

PATRICK: **Help.**
I am trapped here in the audit office.
I am in the audit office.

I stop shouting and listen out for the helicopter, but I can't hear it.
I just have to wait a little longer.

My mouth feels dry. I suddenly realise I'm thirsty.

I wait patiently for a while and wonder how much time has passed. It's still the same day; I'm sure of that. It's very dark; I'm sure of that, and my watch is on my left wrist; I'm sure of that too.

They must have landed and are now looking and listening out for survivors.

(Shouting)

PATRICK: **Help.**
Help. Please.
I am trapped.

(Louder)

Help.

Arrrgggghhhh.

I am exhausted and wait... and wait...
Minutes, hours pass.

(Whimpering)

PATRICK: **Help – Help me. Help.**

No one hears me and my voice is failing me. I am dying. Death is creeping upon and all around me; waiting for me to weaken so that it can claim me.

I hear a noise. I listen tentatively, slowing my breathing.

FX KNOCK KNOCK, KNOCK KNOCK

PATRICK: **Hello.**
Hello.
Who is there?
Can you hear me?

I try to move the objects that lie across my left arm, trapping my hand. It is too heavy. I remember a story I was once told by a friend about people gaining super strength in times like this. People have been reported to single-handedly move cars and run through burning buildings.

But I can't move. I still hold onto the object in my hand and now I think about it it is cold, smooth, steel, and lies between my thumb and index finger. It comes to me suddenly:

PATRICK: **It's – It's the gun.**

I can shoot it. The sound would act as an SOS. People looking for survivors would know someone was in here. I would be rescued.

But how would I explain the gun?
What would I tell people--that I had just come across it?
I should throw it away.
But I may need it. If it gets too much I will end it; turn it on myself and end it.

    FX   ELECTRICAL SPARK

I hear something.
I feel the building move slightly, the rubble, myself amongst it.
This *must* be an earthquake. It wasn't a bomb or an explosion. This was the aftershock.

A light in the room flickers, on and off.

For the first time in many hours I can see my surroundings.
I look down at my legs, which confirm they are trapped. My arm is trapped but I can see what traps it: plaster, concrete, brick, part of a bookcase, books, papers.

    FX   ELECTRICAL SPARK/RUBBLE AND OBJECTS BEING MOVED

I move the objects which trap my left hand, one by one, bit by bit, slowly; for fear that I may disrupt a stacked pile of rubble and cause further restraint or, at worst, death.
I can't move the bookcase, which is resting on everything else, on top of my arm; trapping my hand.

PATRICK: **Huuuumph. Slowly now, slowly.**

              Arrrrggg

At last my arm is free, bleeding and sore but free.

I am able to lift my upper-body up, and off the ground. I gaze at the gun. It seems to change shape in the flicker of the light.

My thoughts return to past events; events I deeply regret. I am not sure if I had killed him.

I waited for him to turn around, to face me. I aimed but did I shoot, did I hit him? It was at that point that I was up in the air, grabbing for something to hold on to.

(Sobbing)

PATRICK: **Lord Jesus, I am sorry for my sins, I renounce Satan and all his works, and I give you my life. I accept you. I now receive and accept you as my personal Lord and my personal saviour, and as we pray, fill us with your holy spirit.**
I am forever your disciple.
In the name of your son Jesus, I pray. Amen.

This prayer is printed on my conscious. It was the prayer that my mother would repeat every Sunday at church. I would ask her why she asked for forgiveness so often; what had she done that was so wrong? But she just prayed harder--more vehemently.

We would go to church every Sunday. I would wear my Sunday outfit; black trousers, that were a little too short but immaculate in every other way and a luminous white shirt.

Mother would wear her best dress. It was white, patterned with multicoloured flowers. Her hair always smelled burnt on a Sunday because of the straightening combs she would heat up on the fire and run through her hair for that neat, slick finish.

My church was a tin shack with a wooden cross, fixed on the top of the archway. It was also my school from Monday to Thursday and my social arrangement on a Saturday.

On Saturdays the local barber's son would hire out time on his Nintendo. Those that couldn't afford to play would huddle around the small TV screen to watch the action; faces lit up a kind of blue-green in the dusk of the evening.

It was in this shack that my life path begun.

I place the gun down on the ground, next to me, afraid not to have it in my intimate possession.

I lean forward and try and move some of the rubble that sits heavy on my legs. I am able to move some but there's a block I just can't move.

PATRICK: **Arrrgggghhhh. Lord, please give me strength. Please don't forsake me. I will forever be your servant if you let me live. Please, let me live to put things right.**

I am not a strong man. I wasn't a strong boy. What did mother used to say? She would say:

PATRICIA: **Patrick, you are a bony, brittle boy but you have a smile that will grant you a place in heaven.**

PATRICK: Like many of the children in my village I spent most of my childhood hungry and undernourished. In desperate times we would have to eat dry biscuits; one of the ingredients soil.

I grab the gun, sit for a moment and ponder my life; thinking about the choices I have made. How had I come to be here – trapped, a murderer. Am I a murderer? Did I aim? Yes. Did I fire? I don't know. I can't remember.

I'm hungry, thirsty and the pain creeps up my legs, teasing at my thighs once again.

FX   ELECTRIC SPARKING

The light is fading now. It won't be too long before I am in total darkness again.
I scan the room, trying to record a mental picture of where I am sitting. I can't see much farther beyond the rubble around me; rocks, iron rods spiralling out of the concrete. I look up and see that the ceiling is gone. I can see two floors above me.

I see carpet on the floor near me. I touch it and it softness comforts me.
To my left are papers and books. I grab a handful of papers and wait for a flicker of light so that I can see the words.

FX   RUFFLE OF PAPERS

The letters I have in my hand show a crest at the top, which I recognise. They are official government papers. They are infact, briefing notes to the ministers.

Most are financial forecasts, budgetary reports.
The figures would have been provided by me and written as a briefing note to the ministers.

I have been working in the government for just over three months now and already, I have gained a reputation most officials would be proud of.

A flush of pride sweeps over me, swiftly followed by dread and regret.

My mother and grandfather would turn in their graves if they could see me now.
I have both to thank for everything.
What have I done? I have ruined everything.
In the space of a few days I had become someone else. This is not
me. I shouldn't be here.

SCENE 5.
IN THE FAMILY HOME

FADE UP

PATRICK: They said I was a gifted child. I could read before I could walk. Mama could not afford to buy books but Haitians are resourceful souls.

> FX. CHILD READING NUTRITIONAL TAG OF A RICE PACKET

I would read everything from the wrapper on a tin can, the nutritional tag on a rice packet to the books my teacher would secretly loan me. My grandfather always said that to read well was the key to the world. You didn't need to leave Haiti to travel across oceans.
If you were able to read, you could travel the world, experience life and death, happiness and sorrow. You could walk with dinosaurs and voyage with pirates.

Whenever he came to visit he would bring me a newspaper and we would read it together. I would be enthralled by the events which would unfold as I read the words.
But I really enjoyed reading stories.

My favourite was Mark Twain's Adventures of Huckleberry Finn. My God, I must have read that book a hundred times and more. My teacher gave me my own copy to keep for reading so well.

> FADE OUT
>
> FADE UP
>
> SCENE 6.
>
> THE TIN SHACK/SCHOOL
>
> FX LOW MURMOUR OF CHILDREN CHATTING

TEACHER: O.K. children. Settle down. Hush now. So we are going to read something this week. I only have the one copy so we will take turns to

The Aftershock — 113

> read. We will pass it around the class and each pupil will take their turn.

PUPIL: But what will happen if we cannot read the words?

TEACHER: That is why we are all here. That is why we go to school to learn how to read the words. No one is able to read first time. It takes practice.

So who will go first?

PUPIL: I don't want to go first.

PATRICK: Me, me. Ma'am. I can read.

TEACHER: O.K. Hush children. Let us hear Patrick try to read.

PATRICK: Sometimes we'd have the whole river all to ourselves for the longest time. Yonder was the banks and the islands, across the water; and maybe a spark — which was a candle in a cabin window — and sometimes on the water you could see a spark or two — on a raft or a scow, you know; and maybe you could hear a fiddle or a song coming over from one of them crafts. It's lovely to live on a raft. We had the sky, up there, all speckled with stars, and we used to lay on our backs and look up at them, and discuss about whether they was made, or only just happened — Jim he allowed they was made, but I allowed they happened; I judged it would have took too long to make so many. Jim said the moon could a laid them; well, that looked kind of reasonable, so I didn't say nothing against it, because I've seen a frog lay most as many, so of course it could be done. We used to watch the stars that fell, too, and see them streak down. Jim allowed they'd got spoiled and was hove out of the nest.

TEACHER: Well done Patrick. You read eloquently. Well done. I'm really impressed. Where did you learn how to read so well?

PUPIL: Patrick is eloquently. Hahaha.

    FX   CHILDREN LAUGHING

    FADE OUT

SCENE 7.
UNDER THE MINISTRY OF FINANCE/ UNDER THE RUBBLE

PATRICK: **What good will figures do me now?**

    FX   CRUMPLE OF PAPER

My head is sore. I touch it unwillingly, anticipating a crack in my skull, exposed brain matter, blood.

I feel a small, sticky gash.

I look at my hand for signs of blood but the light doesn't flicker and I am in total darkness.

I can't sit here and wait to die. I need to try again and move. I place the gun down on the floor beside me, steady myself by placing my hands by my sides, lean back and try and wriggle my legs free. It is no good and only gives me more pain.

(Shouting)

PATRICK: **I will shoot it off.**

    FX BANG BANG/DUST FALLING

PATRICK: The only result is more dust.
I have wasted two bullets.
I pick up the gun, sit still and wait to see if the shots have been heard by anyone.

(Long pause)

I cannot be the only person alive in this building.

(Whimper)

PATRICK: **Hello.**
Can anyone hear me?
I am trapped.
I am in the audit office.

I am fatigued. I want to rest. I lie back holding the gun close to my chest. I will rest for a while and then I *will* get out of here.

    FADE UP

    FX MUSIC

Remembering the song that played on the radio this morning I fall into sleep:

VOCALIST: We are prisoners in our own land
Our children have never seen a living flower
The air we breathe is thick
The water we drink, polluted
Our rivers run of trash

Haiti the orphan land
Haiti the troubled land
Haiti the mother land
We will not desert you
Like many other man

Break the shackles and free yourself
Take a new road
Change your destiny
Your lord will guide you
Believe in him and he will give you the power to break free

Haiti the orphan land
Haiti the troubled land
Haiti the mother land
We will not desert you
Like many other man

SCENE 8.
UNDER THE MINISTRY OF FINANCE/ UNDER THE RUBBLE

PATRICK: I wake--dazed. I am gripping the gun.

I look around but I am still in total darkness. I check the magazine to make sure I still have bullets; 3 left. I place the gun down on the ground.

I am terribly thirsty now but I must try and break free.
I try again to move the rubble that lies heavy on my legs.

> FX RUBBLE MOVING AROUND/HEAVY BREATHING

PATRICK: **Arrrrggghhhh.**

I can't manage to move the bigger pieces.
Something heavy sits on the smaller objects.
It is too dark to see but if I throw a brick at the light it may come back on.

> FX RUBBLE HITTING THE CEILING/
> PATRICK STRAINING

PATRICK: **Yes! Thank you lord.**

Now I need to get more power to my upper body
So that I can push off what is covering my legs.

PATRICK: **Huuummmmmppphhhhh**
Arrrggggghhhh
Huuuummmmppppphhhhh

Something has shifted I feel the pressure on my thighs ease.

> FX ELECTRICAL FLICKER

The light has gone again.

I feel for feeling; hoping I haven't caused more damage to my legs.

PATRICK: **What's this?**

Something rubbery, soft, hard and sticky.
I pick it up but I can't see what it is.

I feel it with both hands, turning it around, upside down.

I smell it but can't sense any odour.
All I smell is the dust of concrete.

> FX ELECTRICAL FLICKER

The light is back on.

I look at the object but even with the light on I can't see what it is. It's dusty and has a metal ring around it.

I muster up enough saliva to spit on it. I brush it clean.

PATRICK: **O' God! No.**

It's a finger.

I recognise the ring. The ring--it's his ring--it's his finger.

I toss it aside. Maybe not hard enough.

It can't be.
I feel around for it, find it and pick it up.
I look at it again; at the ring – to make sure my mind isn't playing tricks on me.

Did I shoot it from his hand?
Was it severed in the earthquake?

I look around.
He could be close by.

    FADE UP

    FX   MUSIC (VOODOO DRUMS)

PATRICK: (Shouting)

Help
Help me.
Get me out of here.
Please, somebody.

    FADE OUT

Sean Pullen

Pouring a small measure of brandy, he lights a cigarette and stares at the keyboard for twenty minutes. There's no such thing as writer's block. He's read it somewhere, or heard it at his writing group. Another small measure, another cigarette, another twenty minutes pass.

Eventually, after several shots, and countless cigarettes, the words flow, and brain to keyboard connect. He closes the laptop with a feeling of accomplishment.

The following day, void of the many small measures, he reads his work - then sinks in despair. Pressing delete he stares at the keyboard. Twenty long minutes pass. He pours himself a small measure, and lights a cigarette.

Falling Away
A memoir
by Sean Pullen

We've been driving forever. I'm starting to wonder if we will ever get there. I've counted every green car and I'm now sick of it. Playing I-spy became tedious as it wasn't much fun by myself and Michael wouldn't take part, telling me I was a girl, as that's what girls do. This didn't bother me, as sometimes I want to be a girl. They don't have to play football, or fight each other, and they can cry and not be called a sissy.

So being a girl isn't that bad.

Eventually Michael falls asleep. I watch dribble slide from his mouth down his chin. When this happens I know he's in a deep sleep and I can wipe my bogeys in his hair.

I do not know when or how, but I fall asleep myself. I know this because when we arrive, dad opens the Cortina's rear door and shakes me so hard I fall out the car landing on the floor.

Mom says I don't need stitches and will probably have a headache later. She wipes the blood away with her spittle on a hanky and kisses the cut on my head. I can't understand how kissing makes it any better. It doesn't, so what's the point.

But I don't care, nor do I cry, because we're here. Butlins. The best place in the world.

We make our way to Reception and then to Yellow camp, that's where our chalet is. Unpacking our suitcases, we then go to the dining hall. The smell hits me as we near the entrance. It smells like the dinners at school and this makes me hungry, as school dinners are the best. Banana custard and chocolate crumble. Just the thought of it, although they do have a bad side - apple crumble and rhubarb.

Dad says he hopes we don't have to queue for our dinner. He says it would be like being in the canteen at work. Dad's canteen must be like my school. I wonder if he gets told off for pushing in too. The noise is tremendous. I'm sure if my headmaster Mr Jenkins was here now he'd be appalled.

We take our seats at the long row of tables that seems to stretch for miles. Me and my brother squeeze between two really old people. The one I am next to is a big lady who sags over the side of her chair. I find myself leaning to the left, unable to sit up straight, as there isn't much room. She glances down, gives me a broad smile as the white powder on her face cracks around her mouth. I smile back.

I'm propelled into her fat flabby arm as my brother pushes me hard.

'Move over you spaz.' The words spit out between gritted teeth. Dad glares at both of us from across the table. He doesn't have to say anything, to me anyway, Just that stare is enough.

Only last week I was washing Teddy Lenny in the toilet bowl. I decided to use dad's razor to give him a shave. Teddy bears don't have beards, but he had fuzzy stuff over his head because he was right old. I know at the age of nine I'm far too old to have a teddy bear, but I have had him forever and I'm not going to give him up, shove him in the attic and forget about him like mom and dad have done with their things. No one really knows about Lenny, cos' if they knew at school, they would call me names and I'd have to fight again. So he's like a secret ted, only coming out at bedtime and when I'm alone in my room. My brother says I'm a homosexual as only homosexuals and girls play with teddy bears. I don't know what a homosexual is, but think they must be OK if they like teddies.

Anyway, dad came in and made me jump, dropping his best razor down the pan. He went barmy at me. He wanted to know what the hell I was doing washing something in the toilet bowl. I tried to tell him that the bath was full of things mom had left to soak and the sink, which he knew, was blocked.

I never got to say that. He swiped me across the ear when he saw his bestest razor at the bottom of the pan. My ear made ringing noises all that day, and Lenny never got his shave.

I finish my dinner and wolf down my blancmange feeling I could eat more. Wish I could have eaten it sitting up straight. Another nudge from my brother, as he guides a large spoonful of something in my direction.

'Want some chocolate ice cream?' he asks smiling. Taking the spoon, I shove it into my mouth. It doesn't taste right. It's not cold like it should be.

I stand up, slamming once again into the fat lady's fat arm as the burning sensation rips through my taste buds and down my throat. I spit out what is left in my mouth and scream. All eyes are now on me. The look of shock and horror on my parents' faces mirrors my own. I turn to my brother, whose smile is now a triumphant grin. Scanning the table I snatch up the glass of water nearest me, gulping down the liquid as though my life depends on it.

I am grabbed, snatched away from where I stand and led outside away from the dining hall and all the staring faces.

I have never tasted English mustard before, and decide I never want to taste it ever again.

It felt like I was choking, that I couldn't breathe. It's like the time I swallowed a pea from my pea shooter. I ran from my room, down the stairs panicking and fell the last four steps landing hard against the front door making Jesus fall off the wall onto the glass telephone table which smashed, causing the telephone to fall to the floor. Jesus got glued but mom and dad had to shout down the telephone after that as people couldn't hear on the other end. I'm glad I did, fall that is, because it dislodged the small dried pea allowing me to breathe again.

Outside the dining hall, dad gives my brother a big hiding. I'm loving it. I haven't seen him cry in ages. Now he is acting like a girl.

With the burning sensation almost gone, all I want to do is go to the beach, have been waiting for months to do so. I ask, then plead, but am told it's too late in the day now and we will go in the morning.

I am devastated, have waited so very very long and now, will have to wait until tomorrow, which is like a thousand years away. I decide to sulk, really sulk, say nothing to anyone for the rest of my life. This is my holiday and as far as I'm concerned, they have spoiled my entire life. I will never, never talk to any of them again.

The clock in our chalet shows half past two. By now I'm fed up with reading Whizzer and Chips and the Beano, and waiting for my dinner to go down. I tell mom I'm bored and that I want to do something. She says we're going out soon to look around. Immediately I throw down my comic and stand by the chalet door quietly jigging up and down like when I need the toilet. My brother sits on a seat, elbows on knees, head in hands staring at the wall. I remember watching a film, it was about monsters from outer space who take over people's bodies. I think that has happened to my brother.

It's since he grew a lawn under his underpants. Mom said he's becoming a teenager and soon he'll be a man. It'll happen to me one day she said. It worries me that I'm going to be like my brother. Get hairs and spots, have my voice sound like a donkey, keep getting into trouble and stop having fun.

Eventually my parents coax my brother out of his seat, aided with some sharp words from dad, and we step out into the bright sunlight making our way onto the big wide path.

My mom stops walking and turns to my dad.

'Maybe we should take them to the beach. The weather may

not be as good tomorrow. It is only a ten minute walk after all.'

'Can I get my trunks?' I ask, already backing away before dad could even answer. Mom turns to look at me. The word 'Yes' falls from her mouth. With that, I run at full speed back towards the chalet slamming into the door. It doesn't open when I pull down the lever. Mom must have locked it.

I wait, watch, as the others slowly make their way back towards where I now stand. Why do they have to be so slow. I start to jig again and mom asks if I need the toilet.

The afternoon sun is getting hotter. I run as fast as I can down the beach towards the sea. Soon the cold frothy water is up to my thighs and I quickly run back out. I can't understand how the sea could be so cold on such a hot day. I venture back in. This time, inch by inch, adjusting myself to the temperature until the waves hit my waist. It's not like it is in the swimming baths. The sea pushes me from side to side. I look up the beach towards mom and dad. They all seem so far away. Michael is sitting with them up by the beach wall. I remember when we went to Ireland two years ago, my brother was the one who couldn't wait to get in the sea. It was him who dragged me into it. I want him to join me, to be like he was in Ireland.

Wrapping my arms around my chest, I look out across the grey water stretching out in front of me. That's where Ireland is. I know that, because dad told me. I turn around to face the beach thinking I'm soon going to get out – it's too cold.

My brother runs across the sand heading towards me. Reaching the water's edge he kicks off his pumps, jeans and socks then races in screaming 'Shit... It's cold...' As he wades further in waves splash up his side before he finally reaches me where I stand, shivering, trying to steady myself. Water pushes around his waist and around my chest. His smile turns to a manic grin as he shoves hard sending me backwards into the frothy water before shouting, 'come and get me if you can.'

I struggle against the tide as Michael moves back to the beach laughing. He's now like the brother I used to know. Before he went strange.

My toes start to hurt. Much like when you walk to school in the snow. Now my bottom half feels like ice. Yet the sun is warm on my back. I decide to get out, follow my brother up the beach to where mom waits with my favourite orange bath towel. Not that it's mine. But it's the one I like to use when I have a bath at home. She wraps it around my shoulders and I head off several feet away to dig a hole in the sand. I look around the beach for something to bury, but there isn't anything. Just sand and sea stretching out before me. There aren't even rock pools here like there are in Ireland where I could look for dead crabs. I fill in the hole then decide to make a sand castle.

When I was little I wanted to be a king and live in a castle. I still think it would be great to do that, be a king – live in a big castle with a moat surrounding it, and have an army at my command. I would order them to capture my brother and torture him, just for fun. Make him say nice things about me, and call me master.

Turning to mom and dad, I want them to see my work. They're both now standing up and dad is shouting at mom. He storms off, disappearing out of sight. Mom raises her hands to her face, quietly sobbing. I know she's crying, I've seen her like this many times before. My brother stares, not knowing what to say or do. I do.

Running over I throw my arms around her. She throws her arms around me, squeezing me hard.

'Come on boys,' she says, her voice slightly cracking as though she had something stuck in her throat, 'let's go back.'

Picking up our towels and clothes off the sand, we follow mom back to the camp. I glance at my brother. An angry frown fills his face, yet I know he isn't angry at mom, or me.

It's seven o'clock in the evening and dad brings mom a cup of tea. She smiles briefly, taking the drink from him. Dad gives an awkward smile back, then mom announces,

'There's a group on tonight in the entertainment hall. It'll be nice to get out for the evening. After all, we are on holiday.'

Dad agrees then looks towards my brother then me.

'Stop that,' he shouts in my direction.

I stop picking my nose and quickly dispose of the contents into my mouth.

Dad grimaces and shouts. 'Don't ever let me see you doing that again. It's disgusting,'

'He's always eating his bogeys,' says my brother staring at me with a grin, glad I have got into trouble.

I am told to put on my bestest trousers, which are now too short as they don't come to the bottom of my ankles any more, put on my new school shirt, comb my hair and wash my face. In the bathroom my brother shoves me to one side, away from the sink.

'Get out the way dickhead,'

He leans forward, pushing his ugly mush in front of the mirror before attempting to squeeze an angry looking purplish red spot on his chin. A stream of fine yellow mush pebble-dashes his reflection. He stands back, grits his teeth and winces. It hurt him. I'm glad.

We sit at a round table and I sip my Coca Cola. Above me, a large ball made up from lots of small pieces of glass reflects slithers of light all around the room. I think how nice it is and wish I had one in my bedroom.

The room is full of noise and people. It reminds me of a wedding I once went to. It was my cousin's. I remember dancing around the floor, weaving in and out of everyone making myself dizzy. When I got too hot I would go and sip from glasses left abandoned on the tables. Some of them tasted yuk, and I wondered how people could drink these, but others tasted quite nice. I know I fell asleep under a table and the next day felt very ill. I was sick all down the stairs.

After that I decided never to do that again and just to drink Coca Cola or whatever mom and dad gave me. I like drinking Cola, as all it makes me do is burp and fart a lot, and I like doing that.

I pull my chair closer to mom as she says the group will be starting soon. The DJ plays In the Summer Time, by someone called Mungo Jerry, then Spirit In The Sky by Norman Greenbum or something, which I love, I've heard it played on the gramophone and the radio in the kitchen lots of times before we came here and asked mom if she would buy it for me.

The DJ announces the group is about to perform. 'A big hand please for Patience.' I clap, not knowing what I'm clapping for. They haven't even done anything yet.

Patience bursts onto the stage, the lights turn from smoky yellow to blue, then red, then green.

Four people, two men and two ladies, break out into song, dancing in formation, moving from the back of the stage to the front. Arms and legs in complete unison. Then one of the ladies screams out, her vocals high above the others. I think her voice is amazing. It's just so loud. When I'm older, I'm going to be a singer and dancer and work at Butlins. Everyone will know me and I'll call myself Scott Marvel. I have always wanted to be called Scott, like Scott out of Thunderbirds. And Marvel because of the comics. I told my brother this and he said I was definitely a homo.

I want people to get up and dance, but no one will. Everyone claps their hands to the songs, and I clap along too. Mom and dad are smiling, occasionally talking into each other's ears.

We walk back to our chalet. I'm tired, yet I don't want to go to sleep. Mom and dad walk behind talking about the group and other things that I don't understand. I catch up with Michael and ask, 'What did you think of the group?'

'They were rubbish,' he says, not really acknowledging me. More as though he had said it to himself.

'No they wasn't,' I answer. 'They was really good.'

Michael likes The Rolling Stones, Black Sabbath and Deep Purple. I like The Sound of Music, Chitty Chitty Bang Bang and Val Doonican. O'Rafferty's Motor Car is my favourite, and Paddy Mc'Ginty's Goat. My brother says there is something wrong with my head and that I should have been thrown out with the afterbirth. I remember when he used to like the same things I did, and that wasn't too long ago. Like I said. I'm sure he's been body snatched.

We're allowed to read for half an hour before lights out. Michael turns on his side and closes his eyes. I pick up my Whizzer and Chips then settle down into the soapy-smelling sheets.

After a while, the pictures and writing start to move about slightly on the page. I know this is because I'm tired and my eyes just won't stay open like they should. I decide to rest them, just for a minute.

It's dark. I sit up and pull back the heavy curtain allowing the light from the moon to illuminate the room then glance out to the world outside. The sky is full of stars, thick clusters filling the blackness above. I have never seen stars so bright, so close. Across from my room, a few chalet lights glow through half open curtains. I wonder if other people have woken up waiting for the sun to rise so they can start the day as well. Putting my wrist to the window, I can just see the face of my watch, the hands point to ten past four. Morning is hours away yet.

I remember when we were in Ireland, we stayed at my auntie's house by the Jetty. On our first night mom came in to our room and told us if we didn't settle down we'd spend the next day in our beds.

Later that night, Michael woke me up, he said he couldn't sleep so I shouldn't either.

He told me a ghost story, about a shark that would come out from the sea and eat people in their beds. I told him to stop, that I didn't want to hear any more, but he wouldn't. He just kept going on and on. I screamed, wouldn't stop screaming until mom came in, which she did.

My brother said I had had a bad dream. I told mom I was scared, that I wanted to get into her bed. She made me lie down, stroked my forehead and told me not to be afraid. I don't remember any more, but remember waking in the morning in wet sheets. I had pissed the bed. Then that was nothing unusual, as I always pissed the bed and still do.

I glance at Michael, hear his gentle breathing, steady and consistent. I want to wake him up, tell him I can't sleep, that I'm not tired. But know he'll go mad, call me something like homo, or Mongol, and if I'm close enough, he'll whack me.

I need to pee, but thinking about the shark stops me getting up. Slumping back into my sheets, I close my eyes.

Nadia Selina

Nadia Selina is currently a student of the Masters in Writing course at Birmingham City University, in association with the National Academy of Writing. She has a Business degree from the University of Central England, and has an undergraduate Creative Writing Diploma from Western Illinois University, USA. It was while studying in the USA that she first explored Creative Writing. This prose arose from the MA in Writing's Qualifying Module, and is based on an adaptation of a French film, *A Very Long Engagement*, set after the War.

A Very Long Engagement
by Nadia Selina

Grassy alpine plains and scenic mountain ranges line the trodden path. You've had a very long journey, but have finally reached your destination. Wandering up the winding cobbled pavement, you marvel at how far you've come under the blistering midday sun. You slip a hand inside your black jacket to retrieve a white handkerchief, and mop sweat off your balding head. Continuing upwards, you enter a small, quaint, sleepy-looking village...this seems familiar... and realise that, somehow, you've come to the place in which you and your wife grew up together, childhood sweethearts! Emile, do you remember the time you were both about ten or eleven, and Félicie dared you to go onto Farmer Jacqué's land?

It was a fresh summer's morning during the school holidays. You'd been playing down by the stream that runs along the back of the village, jumping off a makeshift swing into the water below, submerging yourselves and seeing who could hold their breath for longest, skimming pebbles off the surface, and other merry games.

Morning slowly rolled into afternoon, by which time hunger was beginning to set in. Then Félicie, she was always so bold and full of adventure, that girl was captivating even then, dared you to go onto Farmer Jacqué's land, lure and steal a chicken. Farmer Jacqué left them to roam - said they tasted better, and he was right. She said to kill the chicken and then you'd both eat it together. You weren't sure at all, but she persuaded you, she was good at that, wasn't she? Of course you said yes.

After towelling down and putting on dry clothes, you headed out. It took about fifteen minutes, but when you got there, you both climbed over the four metre chicken wire fence and headed straight for the chickens, giggling like the kids you were.

After what seemed like hours, you saw one, not fully grown, not yet a chick, that had wondered off and was moving in your direction. Hidden behind a large wooden water barrel, you snared it by the foot in the trap you'd both made and twisted its neck. Quite adept for kids, don't you think? With the spoils you both made your escape. Félicie headed home for a knife, some pots, spices, and what not.

You really liked the way she dealt with the chicken, like a grown woman! She wasn't even squeamish about gutting it, though you helped her with that. She washed, cut, seasoned, and cooked that piece of meat, and it was delicious. Even all these years later you remember its mouth watering taste. Yes, that woman – your woman. That's why you can't stop searching for her. That's why you've somehow ended up in this village, and that's why you won't stop seeking until she's safe in your arms, sweet Félicie.

You look up to see Félicie's Aunt Amice hanging clothes out of her shuttered windows. She's looking good for her age.

'Bonjour', you say, 'Tante Amice? M'excusez?' but the response received is the slamming of wooden shutters on freshly washed garments. How rude! You knock on the front door but receive no response. Nevertheless, you must continue upwards. You're hot and in need of refreshment, but don't wish to deviate just yet. More houses are passed without occupants in sight. You must walk in search of someone, anyone to speak to.

Remember your wedding day, and how stunning your woman looked. The wedding almost didn't happen. You had to deal with that Henri, who had an eye on Félicie. Just because he was from a well-to-do background, he thought he could have your woman. Tried to woo her with his gifts of flowers, fine linen, favours and baskets of food for the family. They betrothed him to your Félicie. But she knew where she belonged, sneaked out on a cool moonless night and met you at the stream, where together you both made your escape. Scandalous! You were the talk of the village and remained the subjects of whispering tongues. Returning a year later, you both discovered that Henri had married Félicie's younger sister, Éloise.

Turning a corner, you see three women clothed in fancy attire sitting on a sheer cliff wall, engrossed in conversation. They do not turn as you approach.

'Bonjour,' you say, 'm'excusez?' But they ignore you. Yet again no response. What's the matter with these people, it's like their hearing is impaired. Just move on. Turn on your heels and go in search of people that are more receptive to speak to.

Jacket in hand you leave the village, with its rude inhabitants, and go down a short dusty embankment into a grassy clearing. In the distance you spot a man on a donkey, and as he gets closer you see that he's a monk. Surely he'll help.

'Bonjour' you say again, 'm'excusez? Je suis... je cherche...' But the monk merely rides past, working his way up the embankment, without as much as a glance in your direction.

'Bonjour – m'excusez!' you shout to the retreating figure. This time the response received is fresh donkey shit rolling down to your black leather shoes. Nice! A monk - isn't he supposed to be a Good Samaritan or something and help those in need? Well there is need right here. Walk back the way you came. There's that bistro in the centre of the village. The sun is relentless, the hours of non-stop walking are taking their toll, you need to sit down, refresh and gather yourself before resuming the search. You stop to catch your breath and wipe sweat from your brow. Continuing upwards, you finally see the bistro on the hill top and double your efforts.

Outside a lemon tree shades wooden tables and chairs. You step inside, order a beer and step back outside to sit under the shade. Taking a few sips, you shut your eyes, savouring the cool refreshing liquid as it courses down your parched throat. Your tense muscles begin to relax as the alcohol slowly enters your system.

Then you open your eyes to find yourself surrounded - by three tanned young men with anxious faces. They've actually acknowledged your presence, unlike the others in the village. This makes a pleasant change. But... wait... they look familiar... then the realisation dawns that they're your three nephews. They'll be able to help. They'll help you find your wife.

Remember how over the summer break you'd take them camping in the woods with their father, your brother, and your two sons. You taught them the way to snare animals using the same technique that you used with Félicie on the chicken; a technique taught to you by your father, who in turn was taught by his father. Grandad - he was tough. Here they are, it's them - it's been too long... you've missed them. Brys, Burnel and Romain, your three nephews who died in the War are speaking to you.

Standing to greet them with hugs and kisses, you glance downhill and see a black Rolls Royce, decorated with white tassels, metal objects and a 'Just Married' sign, being chased by a group of young men and boys, saluting the marriage, as is the custom, by firing double-barrelled shotguns into the air.

You wake up in bed, drenched with sweat, and realise it was all just a lurid dream... It was the sound of firecrackers celebrating the New Year that awoke you from your slumber. You're dressed in your starched dark green pilot's uniform, embellished with medals of bravery and honour. To calm yourself, you turn to your wife, who's looking splendid in her wedding gown. Her eyes are closed, skin pale and luminous under the moon's reflection. Looking into her peaceful face you say:

'It's all right mon amour, I've finally found you. I've got you mon amour ... I've got you. I'm never letting you go.'

'Yes mon amour,' is her response 'I've got you too. Just the two of us...'

You kiss her cold lips and embrace her stiffened body.

Francis M. Thomas

Fran "claims" to have written and directed genre-mashing shorts which have travelled the festival circuit, formed part of new media installations and even been broadcast on national TV. Apparently he wrote *Clean-Up* after recovering from a near fatal case of excessive home renovation, it supposedly being an entirely true account of events documented after repeated request by his therapist.

It may be true, but he also professes to own the letter X and spends most weekends protesting at hospital radiology departments demanding delinquent royalties.

Clean-up on Aisle Five
by Francis M. Thomas

INT. LIVING ROOM - DAY

A small terraced living room; a greying Bulldog lies on the sofa asleep, head to one side, legs in the air and drooling. KEVIN, unshaven and thirty-something mirrors the dog; asleep, drooling.

A large TV hangs on the wall above an unopened flat-pack of shelves and a tin of red paint. Somewhere in another room a phone rings distantly.

>PRESENTER (O.S. TV)
>Runcorn FC four, Manchester United nil.

A loud, unusually annoying BEEP of an answering machine wakes Kevin and his dog abruptly.

>WIFE (O.S. PHONE)
>(high pitched, irate)
>Kevin?

Kevin attempts to straighten himself up at the sound of his wife's voice, running a hand through his hair he only succeeds in making it look worse.

>WIFE (O.S. PHONE)
>Are you watching the football?
>(pause)
>Are you asleep?

Kevin looks around the room nervously.

>WIFE (O.S. PHONE)
>I'll be home at five, if you haven't put those shelves up by then I'm cancelling the sports channel!

The phone clicks then DIAL TONE. Kevin looks at

the clock, sees that it's five past four and jumps up energetically from the sofa.

SERIES OF TWO SECOND SHOTS:

A) Rips open the flat-pack using a spoon

B) Lifts a toolbox, tools scatter all over the floor

C) Spills coffee over the instructions

INT. LIVING ROOM - DAY

Kevin, kneeling over the opened pack of shelves, studies the instructions - a pile of coffee stained paper and tools by his side.

> KEVIN
> (to himself)
> Three-quarter-inch screws?

EXT. GARDEN - DAY

Cardboard cartons, old tool boxes and other assorted containers FLY OUT THE DOOR, as inside the shed Kevin searches for some screws.

INT. GARDEN SHED - DAY

Reaching the bottom of a pile of junk Kevin discovers a catalogue for C & R Mega-Super-DIY-Warehouse.

SERIES OF TWO SECOND SHOTS:

A) Finds his keys down the back of the sofa

B) Slams his car door

C) Groans as he waits in a long line of cars in the C & R car park

EXT. C & R CAR PARK - DAY

Kevin glances at the clock on the dashboard; four fifteen. Spying a prime space near the store entrance, clearly sign-posted 'customer parking', he indicates and begins to turn.

A small two-seater car SPEEDS up the wrong way of the one-way system, SQUEEZES past him into his space and KNOCKS OFF his wing mirror.

Kevin leans on his HORN, then exits his car. SENIOR ASSISTANT NANCY, a short blonde girl, mobile phone to her ear and wearing a pink C & R uniform exits her car.

>					KEVIN
> 				(shouting)
> 		Excuse me!?

Kevin picks up the wing mirror and hopelessly tries to re-attach it to the car.

> 			SENIOR ASSISTANT NANCY
> 		It's just a scratch.

Senior Assistant Nancy flashes Kevin a sarcastic smile and hurries into the store.

EXT. C & R ENTRANCE - DAY

Kevin BUMPS into the automatic doors as they fail to open, despite just opening for another customer. A member of staff with a trolley HITS HIM IN THE ANKLES from behind.

> 					KEVIN
> 				(turning)
> 		Seriously!?

The staff member just grins at Kevin. As he approaches the doors they open to let him in.

INT. C & R ENTRANCE - DAY

A stadium sized store, endless aisles disappear with the curvature of the earth.

At the customer service desk an IRATE CUSTOMER argues with an assistant over a refund. Kevin approaches ASSISTANT IAN who is 'greeting' customers by the entrance.

          ASSISTANT IAN
    (monotone, picking his nose)
Hi welcome to C and R mega-super-diy-warehouse please check out our today-only special offers on hoses, green paint, and garden furniture in aisles eighteen, forty seven and one hundred and ninety four -
    (struggling)
- re-spec-tiv-ely.

          KEVIN
Can you tell me which aisle I need for wood screws please?

The assistant shrugs dismissively, stares at him blankly then continues to pick his nose.

INT. C & R DECORATING AISLE - DAY

Kevin passes aisle after aisle searching for the hardware section. Locating another member of staff he approaches ASSISTANT GEOFF who has an OLD MAN & WOMAN practically pinned with their backs to a wall of paint brushes dispensing advice.

ASSISTANT GEOFF	OLD WOMAN
..but if you really care about the brush, it has to be made with..	(mouthing to Kevin) Help.

KEVIN
(interjecting)
Can you tell me where the hardware aisle is please?

Assistant Geoff turns and smiles crazily at Kevin.

ASSISTANT GEOFF
I will answer your question after I have finished explaining the subtle differences between hog and squirrel brush hair to this decrepit pair.

The Old Man squints at Assistant Geoff and tightens his grip on the handle of a new axe, label still attached.

INT. C & R CLOCK AISLE - DAY

Kevin rushes past an aisle dedicated to wall clocks, hundreds of second hands TICK as the time reaches four thirty.

INT. C & R HARDWARE AISLE - DAY

Turning into the hardware aisle Kevin sees a sign for wood screws.

Arriving at the shelf below the sign, all the small tubs which should contain the hardware are empty. Leaning on the shelves nearby ASSISTANT BRAD reads a magazine; Screwed and Nailed Quarterly.

KEVIN
Three-quarter-inch wood screws?

ASSISTANT BRAD
I work on plumbing.

Assistant Brad briefly glances at the other side of the aisle, then goes back to his magazine.

KEVIN
Where are all the screws?

Assistant Brad doesn't respond. Further up the
aisle, dressed in an 'I screw, do you?' T-shirt
ASSISTANT CHUCK reaches deep into a shelf and
pulls out a bag of screws.

> KEVIN
> (from a distance)
> Excuse me?

Kevin approaches Assistant Chuck who hasn't
acknowledged him, he sees that the screws he's
holding are three-quarter-inch!

> KEVIN
> I really need those screws.

> ASSISTANT CHUCK
> (smirking)
> Sorry, they're not for sale.

Assistant Chuck heads up the aisle away from
Kevin.

> KEVIN
> (following)
> What's wrong with them?

> ASSISTANT CHUCK
> (without turning)
> We just did a stocktake, they don't
> actually exist, so I need to dispose
> of them.

Kevin flips, grabs Assistant Chuck by the
shoulders and pushes him up against the shelving.

> KEVIN
> I really, really, need those screws.

Kevin snatches the bag of screws from Assistant
Chuck, lets him go and begins to make his way
back to the checkout. Assistant Chuck pauses for
a moment then picks up a NAIL GUN from a nearby
shelf.

> ASSISTANT CHUCK
> (shouting after Kevin)
> Are you sure you have everything you need, sir?

Kevin looks over his shoulder, stops and turns back to face Chuck.

> KEVIN
> Actually, no. I'm going to need a customer complaint card.

A rabid look crosses Chuck's face then HE STARTS SHOOTING NAILS down the aisle at Kevin.

An innocent couple picking out door handles are GUNNED DOWN as Kevin DIVES behind a display, narrowly avoiding being hit and DROPPING HIS SCREWS; they slide out of reach under the fixtures!

Some smarter customers TAKE COVER, others pick up anything they can get their hands on; PAINT TINS, U-BENDS and DOOR HANDLES are LAUNCHED at Chuck who deflects and dodges the attacks then continues TAKING OUT CUSTOMERS WITH HIS NAIL GUN.

Kevin looks around for a weapon; he grabs a BLOWTORCH, lights it up and waves it in front of him like a SWORD - a metal DUSTBIN LID as a SHIELD.

In a heroic effort to take down the gunman he ROLLS OUT from behind his display and CHARGES at Chuck, NAILS BOUNCE OFF his makeshift shield in every direction.

> ASSISTANT CHUCK
> (shouting over the
> noise of the nail gun)
> I'm afraid we're all out of complaint cards, sir!

He reaches Chuck and points the blow torch at his face. Chuck's hair CATCHES FIRE and he DROPS THE NAIL GUN. Putting his face in his hands he runs away around a corner, SCREAMING LIKE A GIRL.

                    KEVIN
               (shouting after Chuck)
          That's OK, I've decided to take
          matters into my own hands.

A customer stands up from behind a toppled display and CLAPS Kevin enthusiastically.

Other customers begin to emerge from their hiding places as the first guy gets KNOCKED OUT by a flying PAINT TIN; hurled from an unknown foe in the next aisle - the other customers quickly DUCK back behind their defences.

Assistants Geoff, Ian and Brad strut around the corner and line up in the aisle; GLADIATOR STYLE.

Geoff REVS A POWER DRILL menacingly, Ian SWINGS A CROWBAR in complex patterns and Brad holds up a CORDLESS SANDER; the battery dies when he presses the trigger, which he responds to by giving it a shake.

                    ASSISTANT GEOFF
               (menacingly)
          We're here to help.

With a war cry the three assistants CHARGE the aisle, uncovering and SLAUGHTERING CUSTOMERS in poor hiding places as they advance towards Kevin.

Assistant Geoff STABS his drill into a foot protruding from underneath a display door hinged to a shelf. Ian uses his crowbar to SMASH porcelain bathroom furniture and reveal customers as Brad LAUNCHES himself at them, getting his sander caught up in a blonde girl's hair.

INT. C & R WOOD CUTTING AISLE - DAY

News of the battle hasn't reached the aisle. Typical store MOOD MUSIC plays as a number of customers wait to have wood cut by an assistant operating a big machine.

Clean-up on Aisle Five ■ 147

One customer waiting patiently in line has a large piece of wood with a STORE ASSISTANT gagged and strapped to the board.

The in-store announcement tone sounds over the PA system.

> PA MAN (V.O.)
> (completely disinterested)
> Senior Assistant Nancy please report to aisle five, we have a code three. Multiple customers require urgent assistance.

INT. C & R HARDWARE AISLE - DAY

Kevin is now SURROUNDED by Assistants Geoff, Ian and Brad - fully engaged in tool-to-tool combat.

Brad, lying on the floor SANDS KEVIN'S SHIN. Ian SWINGS his crowbar which Kevin BLOCKS using his makeshift shield, PUSHING his attacker over backwards.

Geoff LUNGES; his spinning drill PIERCES Kevin's shield cutting his arm. Kevin cries out in pain and DROPS the lid.

Geoff tries to extract his STUCK drill from the dustbin lid. Kevin KICKS BRAD IN THE FACE, knocking him backwards. Brad's sander CATCHES on the floor and DRAGS him up the aisle, CRASHING into a large stack of paint tins which COLLAPSE and bury him.

Assistant Ian, now back on his feet regroups with Geoff who has freed his drill. Jointly they CIRCLE Kevin just out of reach, preparing to pounce.

> ASSISTANT GEOFF
> I'm going to give you something to complain about, enthusiast!

Seeing the NAIL GUN dropped by Assistant Chuck,

Kevin CHARGES at Ian, TACKLING HIM around the waist. Ian manages to LAND A SWING of his crowbar on Kevin KNOCKING him to the floor, before being knocked over himself.

Geoff RUNS at Kevin as he scrabbles backwards, ARMS FLAILING trying to locate the nail gun. As Geoff is upon him he reaches the nail gun and SHOOTS it at him repeatedly.

Geoff stares directly into the eyes of Kevin before collapsing on top of him; A SOLDIERS DEATH.

Kevin struggles to free himself of Geoff's bulk, dragging himself to his feet he turns to face Ian who's frozen, eyes fixed on the NAIL GUN still in Kevin's grip.

Ian begins to slowly back away as Kevin raises the nail gun.

> ASSISTANT IAN
> How about a ten percent off dining room furniture voucher?

Without flinching Kevin SHOOTS HIM DOWN; behind him the sound of a SHRIEKING CIRCULAR SAW approaches.

Turning about Kevin sees that it's Senior Assistant Nancy WIELDING THE SAW. As she REVS the tool she SWINGS it about her body with MARTIAL ART PRECISION.

Smirking Kevin raises his nail gun and SHOOTS at Nancy. The gun makes a WHIRRING NOISE and recoils but doesn't fire; it's OUT OF AMMO.

Kevin begins moving backwards up the aisle searching for a new weapon as Nancy advances, deftly stepping over the fallen assistants and customers.

Kevin passes the Old Man from earlier, wedged in a gap hidden between the shelves - he glances at the AXE held above his head.

                    OLD MAN
                 (whispering)
        Run.

Senior Assistant Nancy passes the Old Man's hiding
place and the Old Man BRINGS HIS AXE DOWN to meet
her.

Deftly she SWINGS the saw and CUTS THE AXE HANDLE
in two, then BURIES HER SAW IN HIS STOMACH.

Kevin sees a TORRENT OF BLOOD flying out from the
spot where the Old Man was hiding as the Old Woman
runs from her hiding place.

                   OLD WOMAN
        No!

Without flinching Senior Assistant Nancy SPINS
AROUND to meet the Old Woman, DECAPITATING her
easily in one move.

                     KEVIN
        No!

Nancy turns her attention back to Kevin and
continues the advance. Behind Kevin at the exit
to the aisle a number of other store assistants
line up wielding weapons, blocking his escape but
submissively not attacking.

               SENIOR ASSISTANT NANCY
        You should have taken the voucher.

Kevin looks around for a weapon, PICKS UP THE
CROWBAR dropped by Assistant Ian and turns to face
Nancy. Now within range she SWINGS the saw at
Kevin who DODGES AND BLOCKS her attacks with the
crowbar.

Wielding the SAW HIGH ABOVE HER HEAD Nancy brings
it down to meet Kevin's crowbar, KNOCKING HIM OVER
backwards. SPARKS FLY as metal fights metal and
Kevin tries to hold off the weight of Nancy and
her saw.

Kevin's ARMS BEGIN TO WEAKEN and the saw blade lowers; turning his head to the side to avoid the hot sparks he sees the packet of SCREWS he dropped earlier - just out of reach.

> SENIOR ASSISTANT NANCY
> You should have called in a professional.

With a renewed surge of energy Kevin manages to PUSH BACK Nancy, STUMBLING she regains her balance then SWINGS the saw at Kevin.

Timing his counter-attack perfectly Kevin also SWINGS HIS CROWBAR and STRIKES the side of the saw, causing it to continue in its arc back TOWARDS NANCY, SEVERING HER ARM and soaking Kevin in blood.

Nancy DROPS the saw and falls to her knees, in shock she PICKS UP HER SEVERED ARM and whimpering she tries hopelessly to re-attach it before passing out.

> KEVIN
> It's just a scratch. Bitch.

The remaining assistants, seeing their leader defeated LAY DOWN THEIR WEAPONS.

A customer emerges from his hiding place and starts CLAPPING; remembering the previous customers demise he stops and ducks for a moment - no attack comes - he resumes more vigorously.

More customers emerge from their hiding places and join in the applause. Kevin reaches out and picks up his BAG OF SCREWS and standing holds them triumphantly ABOVE HIS HEAD as yet more customers cheer and whistle.

Kevin leans down and lifts up the severed arm of Assistant Nancy to look at her watch, ten to five.

SERIES OF TWO SECOND SHOTS:

A) In the car park he duct-tapes his wing mirror on

B) Throws his keys on the side as he arrives home

C) Drills into the wall as he erects the shelves

INT. LIVING ROOM - DAY

Kevin, still covered in blood paints the successfully erected shelves in his living room red as his Wife arrives home.

                    KEVIN
              (pre-empting)
    I had an argument with the paint.

                    WIFE
    Any problems?

                               FLASHBACK TO:

INT. C & R CHECKOUT - DAY

Kevin tries to SCAN his packet of screws at a self-service checkout, the till beeps negatively. Behind the tills at the customer service desk an Irate Customer with a PNEUMATIC CHISEL in his hands jumps over the counter.

Rubbing the barcode Kevin only succeeds in spreading more blood over the packet. He tries to scan them again, another negative beep.

                               END FLASHBACK

INT. LIVING ROOM - DAY

Kevin pauses from painting the shelves for a moment.

                        KEVIN
    No. Not really.

                                    CREDITS ON BLACK

INT. C & R CAR PARK - NIGHT

Most of the lights are off in the store. Outside the remnants of the customer service team stand in rank with their head's hung low.

Assistant Brad scraped and bruised from being dragged into the paint tins, Chuck with an eye patch from the blowtorch along with Steve and others.

Senior Assistant Nancy moves along the line facing her assistants and in turn rotates her body, slapping each of them in the face with the limp arm that's duct-taped to her body.

                                    CUT TO BLACK

                    THE END

Polly Wright

Polly Wright is a writer, lecturer and artistic director of the arts in health company The Hearth Centre. Tindal Street Press and Diva Press have published four of her short stories, including two in a showcase anthology, edited by Lesley Glaister: "Polly Wright's *Finding Alteration* is the most affecting story, a heart breaking, yet heart warming tale whose economical prose and valiant protagonist speak volumes about teenage love."
-*The Observer.*

Polly has written and directed five plays and her company is in partnership with Birmingham and Solihull Mental Health Foundation Trust and the Birmingham Repertory Theatre.

Delphiniums
by Polly Wright

I wake up dreaming of delphiniums. Blue and fleshy and smelling of ice cream.

A luscious blue scent is filling my head and I am hot and sweaty but when I try to push the downy off, I find that my hands and arms are trapped. Where my hands should be I see little wavy things like the whiskers of prawns.

'Annie,' I shout. Then, hesitantly: 'Help.'

I wait for her to come into the bedroom but all I hear is the slam of the front door.

Silence. No cup of tea. No wee kiss.

All I did was to ask her if she fancied Pat.

'I'm fed up with your jealousy,' she'd screamed. 'You don't own me.'

I start to cry, and then I notice. My tears are sticky.

Perhaps I've had a stroke. Fat lot she cares. Here I am, paralysed and my so called girlfriend has just stomped out the door.

Now I hear the phone ringing. Who turned the bell up so high?

Then it stops and I hear a disembodied voice, like an oracle.

'Hiya, Carol. Just making sure you were coming in the shop today. I'm a wee bit short staffed. You take care, Carol.'

'Ailish!' I shout. And this time with more conviction: 'Help!'

But then a shuddering and clicking sound like a train coming to a halt. And silence again.

But I don't care now because that sharp ice-creamy scent is overpowering me and I am stinking with desire. I slither down the edge of the mattress onto to a steep hill of rough weave which borders a velvet plateau. My sweat eases me along until I come to a sheer white cliff. When I look back I am ashamed to see that I am trailing a rope of silver snot behind me, but I can't stop. The scent is pounding in my head like a blue migraine and I go on, under a bridge which I think might be the window, and there! A great blue tree is waving at me from the flowerbed. I glide down the granite wall of the tenement, so smooth you'd think I'd fall off, but my sweat can cope with any surface. Next, I clamber up the juicy green trunk like a child climbing back up the slide and, yes, nothing can stop me now. I stuff the fleshy flowers into my mouth.

And, oh, they taste like everything I have ever loved. Olives, sweet white wine, Haagen Dass chocolate ice cream and Annie's skin.

*

My first girlfriend fancied herself as a bit of an intellectual. After sex she used to say to say to me:

'Post coitum omne animal triste est,' which she translated: 'After sex all animals are sad.'

After devouring the delphiniums I feel *triste*.

Our garden makes you feel *triste* anyway. Like all Edinburgh gardens, it's sombre and shaded. It's a wonder anything grows, there's so little sun. You can't say anything about it to Annie. She says how lucky we are to have a garden flat. Well, it was her money, so I couldn't really argue. I wanted the attic flat we looked at in Newtown, all angles and light and a glimpse of sea. But no, she had to have her garden of dull shrubs.

'Can't we have some colour?' I pleaded. 'A nice geranium or a Busy Lizzie.' I had imagined potted plants by the back door. She made a *peugh* sound which I was starting to hear a lot.

'Edinburgh gardens are restrained, like the city.'

'OK,' I said. 'How about a delphinium?'

'Buy a delphinium and watch it get eaten by slugs.' she said.

I said: 'What about slug pellets?' Her face became puffy and mean like I imagine her mother looks.

'What about the wildlife? What about Shelagh's cat?'

'And besides,' she went on. 'The garden belongs to the tenement. I went to the last meeting. No plants which attract slugs. End of.' I didn't answer her back. I was beginning not to answer Annie back.

I don't know why, but it really got to me-a building not letting me have a delphinium. I told Ailish at work about it and the next day she gave me one:

'Don't let her control you, hen,' she said.

I took it home and planted it straight away in the flowerbed underneath our window.

And now I have torn that delphinium's leaves to shreds and chomped through its heavenly flowers. The sticky tears start again, but it isn't like crying. More like seeping.

Strong smells are beginning to assault me from other gardens, but I am too tired and too hot to move. I burrow under the heavy soil as if it was sand on a beach. Looking up I can see chinks of sunlight through the furled up leaves of what seems to be a banana tree. I don't remember the tenement allowing tropical plants.

Eventually the shadows steal the flashes of light and it starts to rain. I struggle out of my hole and stretch out so that every pore of my skin can absorb the water.

Then, I feel a sharp pain in my midriff and I look up and see Annie's huge face in the open window frame. She is poking me with a stick.

'Ha ha, Carol,' she says. 'I told you so. Where's your precious delphinium now? In a slug's tummy!'

Sliding up the wall to the window sill, I shout: 'Annie, Annie, it's me! I think I'm ill. My snot is silver and I seem to have got very small. Please ring the doctor. I'm sorry about what I said about you and Pat. I won't ever be jealous again.'

Her face recedes, and she slams the window shut. I think there might be limits to my ability to slide upwards, but the slimy mucous I keep on sweating helps me stick to the glass itself and see into our bedroom.

I see Annie standing with her arms folded looking into a mirror in the corner of the room and brushing her hair slowly, in a sort of abstracted way, without meeting her own eyes. After a moment, she goes and sits on the bed and looks at the phone.

My body tells me I can crawl under the gap between the window and the frame, and, to my amazement, I feel myself expanding and lengthening so I can slither under the wood. On the inside window sill, I have to rest to let my body fatten up again.

But a new smell makes my body stretch with alarm- this time it's smoke. Is Annie setting fire to the flat? Then I see a cigarette in her hand. But Annie doesn't smoke. She's never smoked. She has a glass of red wine too, and looks rather drunk, but I am not surprised by that. She picks up the phone.

'Hi, Ailish.' She says Ail-Ish very carefully, she is trying not to slur her words.

'Was Carol in work today? She's not come home. Oh. I see. Thank you, Ailish.'

After she has put the receiver down she lies on the bed smoking, one arm behind her head. She stubs her cigarette out and lights another one.

'Annie, Annie, I love you,' I shout. Eventually, she falls asleep, without undressing or switching the light off, but I know she's asleep, because her breathing has changed.

'Annie-*please* help me.'

I creep over and under the shiny sill, down the wall, over the soft surface and the rough weave to the gap between the floorboards under the bed. I haven't done this before, but, somehow, I know I can do it. I slither down the dark chasm between the floorboards and, attaching the claw things I have on my stomach, I cling to the splintery underside of the board.

Under the floorboards I'm suspended in a night without stars. There's a whiff of mould from where crumbs have fallen. I have never felt so light. Air has become water and I am floating.

At one point I hear Annie croon: 'My love, my sweet love.'
But I can't hear my name.

*

As soon as I met Annie at the Women and Drumming group, I thought: Emily Jones, from school. Emily Jones was all those top girl things: willowy, beautiful and cruel. She had a best friend called Janet who had green cat's eyes and red hair. They used to stalk the school corridors together, arm in arm, and if you saw them coming you had to flatten yourself against the wall to let them past.

Although they were in the same year as me I didn't think they even knew who I was. But one day they came right up to me in the playground and Janet said:

'You're a worm, aren't you?' Emily Jones stood behind Janet and I could hear her laughing.

My Annie doesn't look like Emily Jones, but she has the same air. When she walks into a room, it is as if she is deciding who is to be her best friend. Of course she has her pick, because she is so beautiful. I knew that if she picked me, I would have no chance. I was still lonely in Edinburgh. I hated the persistent wind and the musty smell of brewing, like damp sacking.

But then, we had to have partners, for the drumming and Annie came and stood beside me. Annie's a social worker, you see, and she loves people who are a bit, well, *inadequate*. She made me listen to the patterns of her beats on the African drum. She tapped the rhythms out on the skin, lightly, and then made me do it. She would listen to my attempts, head on one side, hair over one shoulder, eyes far away. She'd say: 'Not bad,' but I knew I was rubbish.

One day she put her hand over mine and said: 'No- like this.' And when she took her hand away, I could do it. The teacher smiled at me and said:

'That's good, Carol!' Annie drove me home and, as a reward,

she let me kiss her.

I was lost. I knew I would be.

*

Who knows how many days and nights have passed? At night I hang under Annie's bed. Every day I am woken by Annie's alarm and I smell the splintery wood and the mould and then I am lugged by my head into the garden.

The gluey stuff makes it easier to move, but I have noticed, recently, that there are lots of silver trails in the garden, which can't all be mine.

One time I had quite a shock when the tug of my head took me along a trail to some lupins a few gardens away. I slid and slithered towards the flowers, when I slapped, hard, against a wall of cold grey flesh. I shrank back into myself and lay, trembling in the herbaceous border for a while, but in the end I went up close to look at the thing which was barring my way. It was like an enormous dead seal and stank like rotten fish. There were blue cubes spangled all over its slimy body.

I have stopped going to other gardens now, because of the blue cubes. I am not sure, but I think they are dangerous. In the daytime I lie in the nearest flowerbed to our flat. Annie never comes in the garden now. It's sad to see that it's becoming overgrown. I'd help her out, but my head doesn't pull me to weeds.

At night I wrap my belly legs round the window's sash cord and watch Annie. I hear her phone calls about me.

'She just went out one morning and never came back. I'm so sorry, Mrs Stott.'

Then, 'Is that the police? I'd like to register a missing person.'

One evening she comes in earlier than usual carrying some boxes. She opens my wardrobe for the first time since my disappearance and lays the jackets carefully over both her arms. She smoothes their plastic dry cleaning covers before laying them out on the bed. She folds the jeans neatly and arranges my shoes in a line on the floor.

She sits on a chair in the corner and smokes. We both stare at my clothes. Me clinging onto the rough sash cord, her from her wicker armchair.

Eventually she stands up and tugs my favourite jacket out of its plastic bag. It is watery-green velvet, with a black collar and cuffs, and slightly fitted at the waist.

She puts it on. Standing in front of the mirror she bunches her dark hair over one shoulder- and then half turns away and looks at her back. Then she puts on her slinkiest, most swingy skirt, and green suede high heels which I have never seen before. We both stare at her reflection in the mirror.

The phone rings.

She walks towards it slowly, swinging her hips. Does she know I'm watching her?

'Hi, Pat,' she says. Then she says: '7 o'clock. That'll be grand.'

I nearly fall off my hairy rope.

*

It was me who spotted Pat first, because of the way she danced at the Friday night women's discos. She would stand for a long time, watching the scene, before she'd make her way onto the dance floor. The ultraviolet light would pick out her white trousers, white tennis shoes and white teeth. She was always tanned, even in the middle of an Edinburgh winter.

She usually had some rather brassy looking woman in tow, but she was sent ahead to buy the drinks, so Pat could make her entrance. Eventually Pat would slouch onto the dance floor, jutting her pelvis forward as she walked, leather jacket hanging lightly on her shoulders. She would lean back slightly and draw her dance partner to her, so their groins were touching as they swivelled and turned together as if they were doing a tango.

She wore a heavy gold ring on her little finger.

At first Annie and I giggled into our white wine Spritzers about her, but Annie stopped laughing and started ogling. One night, while we were dancing to Annie Lennox, Annie tripped and fell into them, and said:

'Sorry I'm totally pished,' in her mock Scottish accent, which was very embarrassing because Pat *is* Scottish.

Pat did a long draw on her cigarette and narrowed her eyes, as she took in Annie's beauty.

'You enjoy yourself, hen,' she said.

*

A head tug drags me off the sash cord. Like the first day, the blue scent floods my head. I am surprised to find my head pulling me to the kitchen. I have not been there since I have become small, but I have to go. I flatten my slimy skin nae bother, to go under the kitchen door over the wooden floor boards to the table. Blue, blue, purple and blue. A bunch of cut flowers in a vase. Tall, wavy flowers, enticing me. Let me have them. Lupins and delphiniums. Delphiniums and lupins.

Then I see Pat and Annie. Pat is arranging the flowers in the vase, and Annie is drinking wine at the table.

'She hit me and the next morning she walked out. I haven't seen her since,' Then she screams: 'Ugh! Oh.My.God!'

Pat's face comes over the edge of the table, blotting out the pretty flowers. A handsome, tanned face.

'See you-you big fat sluggy. See this!'

I see the great rubber sole of her immaculate tennis pumps coming at me.

'No!' shouts Annie. 'No. Let me look at it.'

She crouches down and her blue eyes are as close as when we used to kiss.

'That explains all the silver trails I keep finding on the carpet.' Pat says: 'How disgusting.'

I hate her. I have grown to love my silver threads. They feel to me like magic threads in a fairy story which wind you safely home.

'I think slugs are rather beautiful,' slurs Annie.

'I've heard everything now,' says Pat. The grooves in her soles are like deep valleys.

'Wait a sec,' Annie says and her face goes away. She comes back with a piece of card she has torn off a Weetabix packet.

'Here, slug,' she says. 'Up you get.'

I am shoved onto the card and lifted up high so I am looking down on the delphiniums and lupins.

'You're going walkies,' Annie says. My little belly legs scrabble on the smooth surface of the Weetabix platform and it is hard to cling on. Before long, however, we are outside and I am pushed off, gently, into wet rich soil.

So- it is confirmed. I have not had a stroke. I have not got MS.

I am a slug. I am no better than that vile corpse slumped beside the lupins, covered in the blue cubes.

*

'D'you know why you're a worm?' Emily said.

I shook my head.

'Because a worm has the sex organs of a male and a female. We did it in biology,' said Janet.

'They're herm-aph-rodites. Like you,' said Emily.

They jabbed me with their forefingers.

'Is it a boy? Is it a girl?' said Janet.

'No- it's a worm!' they cried together and ran off.

From then on, wherever I went, at school and, outside, on the street, I would hear voices. '*Carol Stott is-a-worm.*'

Or just whispers, so quiet I had to turn round to check. There they'd be. Emily and Janet, Janet and Emily, laughing and sitting so closely entwined it was as if they had become the same person.

*

Night falls and the light comes, over and over again. I hardly move from my soil bed. I can feel mites under my skin, crawling and wriggling, but I have no way of getting rid of them.

I am dreaming of hostas. Ribbed and green, with a wavy cream border. I know they are somewhere near. A long long time ago, I didn't think hostas had a scent, but now I know they smell like jasmine, like the crushed petals of pale pink dog roses. I yearn for them and know that I cannot resist the head pull. They are somewhere at the end of next door's garden, I think, under the oak, down among the ferns.

Hostas are the Annies of the plant world. Their beauty is subtle and feline. If hostas had faces they would be hers. I remember how Annie used to take me to the Hermitage in the evenings after Drumming and we'd sit on a bench until the sky turned gold and grey and then dark. It was summer and the heavy smell of lavender and nicotiana surrounded us. I would watch her profile as the shadows darkened her face into silhouette. Her bony nose. The jut of her mouth and the long stretch of her neck.

*

Who knows what time of year it is now? But today I am warm under the soil. It is not raining and not night time, so I have no reason to leave my bed.

Suddenly my head tugs me in the direction of the tenement.

Annie is wearing my green jacket and the swingy skirt. She has put her hair up and she's wearing scarlet lipstick. Pat is wearing her usual get up. Leather jacket. White trousers. She is holding a bottle of wine and brandishing the opener. The silver screw glints in the sun. Music is coming from somewhere.

'Carol was all right really. Just madly jealous.' Pat sloshes the wine into her glass and Annie takes another drag of her cigarette

'And violent,' she adds.

Pat goes off somewhere. Annie croons to the song and stretches her neck up to the sun and half shuts her eyes.

'I was never violent, Annie,' I shout. 'And you know it.'

When Pat comes back she shakes the compact cubes like blue dice round the roots of the delphinium while Annie's eyes are shut.

Slowly I crawl towards the pot. I know what I am going to and I am glad of it.

As I roll in the dice, I watch Pat take Annie by the hand and I see there is a small blue stone set into her heavy gold ring which flashes like a distant glimpse of sea. Not quite, but nearly the same blue as delphiniums.

I look up at Annie's sublime profile, dark against the sun.

Slowly Pat and Annie start to dance, Pat's white groin pressed against Annie's skirt. Together they are like a monstrous green and white insect. Four legs. Four arms. Two heads.

Suzanne Wright

Suzanne Wright's first novel is *The Love Child's Mother*, which is about adoption and reunion. She also has a small volume of short stories, *Intarsia*, the common theme of which is the female experience, and has short stories in two anthologies, *The Spiral Path* and *Finding a Voice*. She is currently working on a novel about the experiences of a single, sixty-something female and her search for love in the post-internet society, and on a one-act play to be performed at the Birmingham Drama Festival in 2012.

The Skeleton in the Cupboard
by Suzanne Wright

She'd gone and died.

Ever since he could remember Granny had been their Christmas visitor. Sometimes Mum's brother or sister came as well, bringing his cousins. Then they had a fantastic time, running about and screaming, playing with the new toys. But they only came for a day. It was Granny who stayed and slept in the spare room, hanging her cardies and blouses and skirts in the cupboard and putting all her jars of cream, comb and make-up on the chest of drawers.

Then she'd gone and died.

They all cried, but Dad had been very, very upset. He'd stood by the big bay window in the bedroom with Will and Sam and explained that Granny had gone to heaven to be with God. His voice was all funny.

William had stood there with his Dad. He felt his sadness, like a big grey blanket, so he reached out and took his Dad's hand in his and squeezed tightly.

'Is she up in the sky?' asked Sammy, and snuffled the snot up into his nose. Disgusting.

Dad got a tissue and blew Sammy's nose.

'Yes –up there above the clouds,' he said. William thought he saw a tear on his cheek. 'She's with Jesus.'

William gazed at the clouds – grey, low, leaking rain. It didn't look like a nice place to be. But his Dad was sad, which made a big lump in his own chest.

'Yes,' he said, 'yes. I think I can see her feet.' He nodded his head wisely.

His Dad squeezed his hand.

'Thanks mate,' he said gruffly.

Mum and Dad had gone to the funeral and Will and Sam had stayed with Auntie Mandy for a day and a night. She'd let them make biscuits, and they slept with Andrew and Charlie. It was OK. They'd had a pillow fight, and Auntie Mandy didn't mind.

When they came back, Dad was very quiet. He wore a white shirt and a dark suit, which Will had never seen before. It looked a bit tight, and his face looked even paler than before. Will gave his Dad a really big hug to cheer him up, then showed him a dead spider he'd found and put in a plastic bag.

Two weeks before Christmas he was in the bath with his brother and his Dad was washing Sam's hair - he was pouring water into the plastic water mill stuck on the side of the bath, making the wheel race faster and faster.

'How long before it's Christmas, Dad?'

'Two weeks. And we've got a special visitor this year,' he replied, soaping Sammy's hair. Sammy didn't mind having his hair washed – he didn't even mind the bubbles in his eyes.

'Who's that then?' asked Will.

Dad continued to soap Sammy's hair as if he'd forgotten the question. Sammy began to squirm because he'd been doing it for about five minutes; he wasn't paying attention.

'Dad. Dad. Who's the visitor then?'

'What? Oh sorry. The visitor. Yes. Big secret mate, a surprise. Wait and see, hey?'

That night, after he'd gone to bed, he could hear their voices from the kitchen. Sammy was asleep. He was only little whereas Will was five, much older.

Will climbed out of bed, crept down the ladder like a tiger and sat on the stairs. They were talking about the funeral.

'I didn't think he would be there,' said Dad.

'Well, they were together for quite a time,' his mum replied. 'Do you remember him?'

'Only vaguely. He was gone by the time I could remember things. I was about Will's age.'

'He came a long way to come to the funeral,' said mum. 'Wonder how he knew.'

'I think Auntie Clair must have told him. She was the only one who kept in touch with him as far as I know. They didn't have any other brothers or sisters, no other family. He never came back, until now.'

William shuffled on the stairs. His bum was going numb and he was cold, and didn't understand the conversation.

The cold was getting into William's nose. It tickled. William struggled against it, and pinched his nostrils shut.

'He was nice. Not what you'd expect from a skeleton in the cupboard,' said mum.

'I think I can understand why he didn't keep in touch,' said dad. 'He thought it would be better to have a clean break, stay out of my life. How wrong can you be?'

William sneezed. It was all the louder for being suppressed. The force of it filled his ears.

The kitchen door swung open sending a slice of yellow light into the hall.

'What are you doing there? Come on mate, bed.'

His Dad gathered him up into his strong arms and placed him gently into bed, tucking the duvet round his shoulders.

'Dad. Who's a skeleton?'

'Don't you worry about skeletons,' his dad said. 'Maybe you'll meet him at Christmas.'

Since then William had given some thought to this idea. Skeletons were dead people, or their bones. He knew quite well what a skeleton looked like. There was a plastic one at playschool, hanging from a hook in the corner of the hall. You could shake hands with it, and that made it rattle, and if you asked Mrs. Young she would tell you what all the bones were called. He wondered if his granny was a skeleton.

When people came for Christmas, you bought them presents. You chose something they would like – things to eat, or wear, or play with. He hoped that this year he was going to have a new two wheeler bike, with a helmet and stabilisers. He'd play with it in the garden, and his Dad would take him up the park to teach him to ride it. Sammy still only had a three wheeler. What could you buy for a skeleton? What did a skeleton want for Christmas? Maybe a beanie, because your head would be cold if you had no skin on your body.

He wondered if the skeleton would sleep in the cupboard. They could move the empty coat hangers along, and put a special hook in there to hang him on. Or maybe put a duvet in the bottom. Perhaps they didn't sleep at all.

He wondered about next door's dog. Flossie was very fond of bones. He'd seen her when Mrs. Crooks gave her a big marrow bone. First she'd sniffed it all over then had a good chew on it. Then she'd taken it out to the rose bed, and buried it. Next day she'd dug it up and given it another chew, then buried it again. Every day she'd done that, until she lost interest and the bone stayed buried in the garden.

What if she took a fancy to their skeleton? They'd have to keep an eye on her, and make sure she didn't get in the house.

Maybe the skeleton would be cold at night. He would get his hot water bottle, and put it in the bed. Or the cupboard.

* * *

William woke suddenly full of excitement and listened to the silence of the house before he remembered; wow, Christmas Day. The special visitor, the skeleton must have arrived last night after he'd gone to sleep.

His brother, Sammy, lay asleep in the bunk bed below him. Mum said Sammy was a snuffly mouth breather. That meant you could always tell when he was asleep.

William peered over the edge of the bunk. There were two

knobbly Christmas sacks on the Tigger rug with blue and green and red and gold wrapped shapes peeping out at the top.

He edged down the ladder and looked closely at the presents, picked one up and shook it. Then he put it down and crept across the room and silently opened the door. He paused to listen. No sound. Along the landing the spare room door stood ajar.

Behind that door lay a secret.

He glanced at his parents' bedroom and heard his dad turning over in bed.

He badly wanted to go back, wake Sammy, and start tearing the paper off the heap of presents.

But even more, he wanted to open this door.

He imagined entering the spare bedroom, opening the cupboard, and seeing the skeleton for the first time.

The bedroom was dark, like an animal's den. William's eyes adjusted to the gloom. Should he look in the cupboard first? What if it was a real skeleton? What if it spoke to him?

Granny's usual neat presence in the room was missing but there was a pile of clothes on the floor, a great big knobbly grey rucksack, and enormous shoes like boats. On the chest of drawers was a small flat book, cigarettes and a lighter, and some money. Her smell, of rose perfume, was replaced with a faint sweetish smell, like in the tobacco shop.

There was a huge hump in the bed, which looked even bigger because he was used to seeing Granny and she was fairly small, and hardly made any difference to the shape of the duvet. William's eyes travelled up the hump to the top. There, between the duvet and the pillow was a head. It had untidy grey hair and a beard.

The eyes opened. They were blue, nearly as blue as dad's and his own.

'You don't look like a skeleton. And you're in the bed, not the cupboard,' said William.

'Hello there. You must be William.' The voice was deep and

sounded different, the words were said in a funny way. 'Pleased to meet you mate. I'm your granddad. I've got a present from Australia for you. Come and say hello.'